THE **HARDY BOYS**®

#174
HIDE-AND-SNEAK

FRANKLIN W. DIXON

Aladdin Paperbacks
New York London Toronto Sydney Singapore

First Aladdin Paperbacks edition August 2002

Copyright © 2002 by Simon & Schuster, Inc.

ALADDIN PAPERBACKS
An imprint of Simon & Schuster
Children's Publishing Division
1230 Avenue of the Americas
New York, NY 10020

The text of this book was set in New Caledonia.

Printed in the United States of America
2 4 6 8 10 9 7 5 3 1

THE HARDY BOYS and THE HARDY BOYS MYSTERY
STORIES are trademarks of Simon & Schuster, Inc.

Library of Congress Control Number: 2001098778

ISBN 0-7434-3758-6

The Object of the Game

"This is the McGuffin," Zack announced.

"And what's that?" Trisha asked.

Zack smiled. "Whatever caused the mystery or action in Alfred Hitchcock's films, he called the McGuffin. It could be a clue, a person, an event—"

Or a really ugly thing, Frank finished for him silently.

"In our film this is what you'll be looking for," Zack said. "First you'll have to find it; after that you'll be searching for whichever team has gotten hold of it. Tomorrow evening bring your boats to the Bayport Marina. You'll get a package of charts and . . . other things that should lead you to where the McGuffin will be hidden. Find it, keep hold of it for three days, and bring it—well, clues about what you should do with it will be in the package for you too."

The Hardy Boys Mystery Stories

Available from MINSTREL Books and ALADDIN Paperbacks

Contents

1 A Star Is Born?

"Exactly what part of 'no' don't you understand?"

Frank Hardy didn't even have to open the door into Mr. Pizza to hear his friend Tony Prito's shout. The pizza place was unusually silent. All the customers seemed very intent on the sodas or slices in front of them while Tony glared at Chet Morton.

"But Tony," Chet said, waving a newspaper, "you've got to admit it's a great chance!"

"Great chance for *what*?" Joe Hardy asked, his blue eyes glinting. "Is another pizza joint offering cheaper prices?"

"I wish," Tony said with a sour look at Chet. "It's a chance to act in a movie."

Joe lost his grin. "Oh," he said in a flat voice. *"That."*

Frank smiled. Since Chet had won a walk-on role in a hot science fiction TV series, *Warp Space*, he'd been bitten by the acting bug. He believed his role as the Slayer from Sirius had opened the door to a whole career.

Frank had thought it was harmless enough. He'd even suggested some local theater groups where Chet might try out.

But Chet thought little theater was beneath him. He kept talking about a movie role. That hadn't seemed likely to happen around Bayport. But it seemed Frank was wrong.

"It's right here in the *Bayport Alternative*." Chet held up the crumpled newspaper. "Some film students are shooting a project here in town, and they're looking for local talent."

"And you want Tony to back you up?" Joe asked.

"He wants me because these people want local talent with *boats*." Tony stifled a yawn. "I'm still trying to wake up, and Chet keeps pestering me."

Frank took in his friend's red-rimmed eyes and droopy eyelids. "Trouble sleeping?" he asked.

Tony shook his head. "More like trouble staying awake. My dad has me playing junior night watchman at this building site. He's a subcontractor on a big job—"

"So big he's got you working as a security guard?" Joe asked.

"Some of the guys think they've seen something," Tony said. "Dad wants to keep it in the family until he has proof."

Frank leaned forward. "What is it?"

"Supposedly they saw someone on the site after they'd locked up and were driving away," Tony replied.

"Want us to lend a hand—or a couple of extra eyes?" Frank said.

Tony shook his head. "I've spent the last couple of nights on this," he said. "Nothing's happened. *Nada.*" He laughed. "You'd have a better time helping out Chet here. After all, you guys have a boat."

Chet's round face lit up with sudden hope. "That's right!"

The *Sleuth* was an older-model Chris-Craft boat that Frank and Joe had bought with their own earnings and some help from their dad. Although summer vacation had already started, they hadn't gotten around to getting it out of the boathouse yet.

"What kind of movie are these people making?" Joe asked.

Chet examined the newspaper. "It doesn't say. Just that they'll be shooting on the bay."

"Shooting on the bay," Joe repeated with a glance

at his older brother. "I'll bet there's a pretty good chance that there'll be pretty girls in bathing suits involved."

Frank could see which way things were going. He raised his hands in surrender. "All right," he said, "I'll dig the *Sleuth* out of mothballs. But you guys will have to help."

"Fine," Joe agreed, "provided we get into the movie." He turned to Chet. "What are we supposed to do to audition?"

"There's a number to call, and they'll set up a meeting," Chet said. "Oh, and they want a photo."

Joe raised his head to show his profile. "What do you think?" he asked, turning his head. "Right side, left side, or straight on?"

Chet took another look at the ad. "Um, actually, they want a picture of the *boat*."

Joe insisted that they send in a picture that at least showed the boys as well as the *Sleuth*. After three days Frank's younger brother was getting as crazed as Chet over not receiving a response to their call. Frank tried hard to rein both of them in. He reminded them that just answering the ad didn't guarantee them parts in this movie. Frank also refused to take the *Sleuth* out of the boathouse until they heard from the film students.

On the fourth day Frank came into the Hardy house and was almost tackled by Joe. "Where've you been?" Joe demanded. "Chet called! The film people want to meet us. It's all set for tomorrow."

"Okay." Frank shrugged. "Did they say to bring anything?"

"Like what?" Joe asked.

"Like a sedative," Frank replied. "If you and Chet are going to be this hyper, you'll sink us before we even get in the boat." Frank smirked at his brother.

The meeting was going to be in one of the classroom buildings at the university. Frank and Joe picked up Chet at what Frank thought was a ridiculously early hour. But when they got to campus, they found this was the day students were clearing out their dorm rooms. The campus was overrun with cars, and it took awhile for them first to find a place to park and then to reach their destination.

Even with the traffic jam, Chet worried about not being on time.

"Chill out," Joe finally said. "Everyone else coming here will have the same problem." Joe was obviously past being starstruck. Frank didn't know whether to be glad or worried at his brother's change of heart.

"I don't think that's the reason for this jam-up." Joe rolled his eyes. "We may be the only ones coming."

That only set Chet off worrying again. As soon as they got into the right building, Chet veered off down a side corridor toward the men's room. "Got to check that I'm looking my best."

Now both Hardys rolled their eyes. "Could we have the letter you got?" Frank asked. "We'll try to find the classroom where we're supposed to be going."

Chet's answer was prompt. "Room 107." He had it memorized!

Frank glanced at Joe. "Don't you want to make sure your hair is okay?"

"Shut up," Joe replied.

They headed back to the main corridor, looking at room numbers. A slim girl with curly black hair came walking toward them, carrying a pile of papers.

"Excuse me," Joe said, giving her a smile. "We're looking for room 107."

"For the film?" the girl asked.

Both boys nodded.

She held up her papers. The top one was a sign: FILM MEETING SHIFTED TO ROOM 234.

"Thanks," Joe said. "Will we see you there?"

"Later," the girl said. "I have to post these first."

They headed for the stairs and encountered another girl. This one had sandy-blond hair and thick-framed eyeglasses perched on a snub nose. She carried a clipboard.

"Here for the film?" she asked. "Room 107 is down this way."

"I thought the meeting was shifted to the second floor," Frank said. "This girl—"

"I don't think so," the girl said. "I'm the writer on the project."

She paused. "And I'm also the the only female on the production team."

2 Mystery Movie

Joe and Frank exchanged a quick look. Could this be some sort of interview test?

"Maybe we misheard," Frank said with a smile. *But I'll certainly be keeping my eyes and ears open from now on,* he promised himself.

Chet Morton came rushing down the hallway. "Did I miss anything?"

Joe shook his head. "I think you're just in time for the excitement to begin." They followed the girl with the clipboard to Room 107.

She opened the door to reveal a classroom with three girls sitting in the front desks—a blonde, a redhead, and the slim brunette whom Frank and Joe had already encountered.

"Nice to meet you," Joe said as if they'd never met before. "I'm Joe Hardy, this is my brother, Frank, and that's Chet Morton."

The dark-haired girl stared at them with her mouth open, not sure what to say. But the girl sitting beside her had no problems thinking of things to say. She was tall, with auburn hair and a gorgeous tan. "As I said in our letter, we were hoping to get a look at the script, or at least the film treatment, before this meeting," she said sternly to the film student with the clipboard.

Her dark-haired friend shook her head, making her curls bounce. "I told you to find out what the deal was before we got here," the brunette said, and turned to the boys. "Hey, this is Willow Sumner. I'm Trisha Eads, and our blond friend is Christy O'Hara. Willow wants to be a movie star. The rest of us are just helping out." Trisha shot a look at the boys as she said this.

"I'm Melody Litovsky," the girl with the clipboard said. She pushed her glasses up on her nose and consulted a short list on the top sheet.

"Okay. We've got the Sumner group."

I guess Willow has enough ego to be a movie star, Frank thought as Melody took a pen and made a check mark.

"You're Morton and friends?" Melody asked

them, glancing from her list to the boys.

"And friends?" Joe had some thoughts about Chet's ego.

But Frank had just gotten a glimpse at how short Melody's list was. "Wait a minute," he said, peering. "Are we all there is?"

Melody's face went pink. "There's one other group. They're late."

"Only one more?" Trisha shot a glance at Willow, who shrugged.

Suddenly Trisha shot up from her seat. "'Scuse me a minute," she said, looking embarrassed.

Melody probably thought Trisha was headed for a bathroom. Frank suspected she was scampering off to get rid of her room-changing signs.

Willow ignored her friend's dash for the door. "What about the script?" she demanded again.

Looks like she's read too many newspaper stories about stars getting approval over the films they're supposed to act in, Frank thought.

Melody's face turned beet red. "Zack, our director, will explain everything," she stuttered.

Frank couldn't help noticing that Melody looked a little upset. Was there a problem with the script?

"I don't think that's very professional," Willow said. "We always have four weeks of rehearsal when we put on a show at Shore Point High."

Shore Point was a town down the coast. *The filmmakers' ad must have traveled pretty far,* Frank thought.

"Trisha and I had the lead parts in the last two plays," Willow added. "Christy does musicals."

Christy nodded. With Willow around, Christy didn't need to do much talking.

"I was in the Shore Point Players' production of *The Miracle Worker,*" Willow said. "We had six weeks of rehearsal there."

Frank looked at the girl with new respect. He'd seen that show. Now he recognized Willow as the wild young Helen Keller in the play.

"And all of us attended Professor Davies's Summer Acting Workshop here at the university." Willow poked Melody. "Although he was talking about stage productions, he said the minimum rehearsal time—"

"When I was on *Warp Space,* we needed only about twenty minutes to rehearse my scene." Chet interrupted. "Of course it took a couple of hours to get the makeup right." He gave Willow the superior smile of a seasoned television actor. *Chew on that, amateur girl.*

Willow gave him a look most people would only use on worms—ugly, unprofessional worms.

Frank hid a smile. If Willow got this kind of

response out of the normally easygoing Chet, this was going to be a very interesting film.

He glanced over at Joe, who was following the byplay. Well, at least there'd be pretty girls in the film. But they obviously didn't play nice.

Trisha came back, carrying several crumpled-up sheets of paper, which she tossed into the classroom's trash can.

A moment later the door opened again. "Everybody here?" a voice asked.

Melody shook her head. "One team—"

"We'll start without them." The voice interrupted.

Frank blinked at the first person who entered the room. The woman in the business suit matched the tone of the voice he'd heard—brisk and confident—as she went to sit behind the instructor's desk. But he'd have sworn he'd heard a male voice.

The person who followed was male, a tall, skinny guy with a narrow face. He joined Melody to stand by the desk as the clear owner of the voice made his entrance. "Hi, everybody. I'm Zack Harris. Why don't you kids take a seat?"

Zack had an animated, sharp-featured face tipped with a little brush of a goatee. With his bright red hair, he looked a little like a cartoon fox. "I'm directing the project. Ms. Joan Athelney is our producer."

The seated woman nodded, running one heavily jeweled hand along her gold necklace.

Now we know where the money for this thing is coming from, Frank thought.

"Leonard Kerwin is director of photography, and Melody Litovsky is doing research and scripting."

Neither of the other two students said a word.

Zack Harris gave his audience a big, toothy grin. "And you guys, and girls, are going to be our actors." *His voice has the same friendliness as a used-car salesman's,* Frank thought.

"I really look forward to working with you, and working hard, because at the end of the coming five days, we'll have made a movie."

A small cheer came from Willow and her friends. Frank could understand that. They had been expecting weeks of rehearsal. Frank knew that film had a more rapid pace than stage plays, but five days?

This was moving way faster than he'd expected. He'd come here to find out if he, Joe, and Chet would even be involved in this film. Not only did Zack take that for granted, he expected them to be done in less than a week!

"H-how do you figure—" Willow started to speak.

"And you are—" Zack interrupted.

"Willow Sumner," Melody quickly said, rolling back some pages and holding out her clipboard. "She and her friends took the Summer Acting Workshop with Professor Davies."

Zack glanced at the board. "So, Willow, did Davies do much improv with you?"

Frank knew the word was theater slang for "improvisation." His parents had taken him to New York to see improv performances at which actors came up with characters, scenes, and dialogue from following suggestions called out by the audience. There were even TV shows that used the idea to create skits and scenes.

But a whole movie improvised?

"We did some class exercises," Willow said warily.

"Then you know how it works. We'll put you in a situation, and you'll have to work your way out of it. You won't even have to act, just be yourself."

For the bossy Willow, that might be a drawback, Frank thought. But he couldn't help watching Melody Litovsky as Zack spoke. No wonder she'd looked upset when Willow demanded to see a script. An improv film wouldn't need a script—or a scriptwriter.

Frank began to think the behind-the-scenes story might be more fun than the actual movie. He looked at the three students and could almost write the plot himself. Melody and Kerwin had probably hooked up with Zack, figuring his fast talking would make it easier to get some money to make their film. To judge from the amount of jewelry on Ms. Athelney, Zack had found a rich producer, but . . .

"Our budget will allow us to shoot for three days." Zack's smile got even bigger. "That should give us enough footage to make a feature-length film!"

There it was, Frank thought. Most student projects were short films, twenty minutes or so. Zack wanted to create something four times as long.

I bet he had to dump his friend's script to do it, Frank thought. He looked over at Kerwin's tight expression. *Something isn't making him too happy either.*

"So why did you need us to bring boats?" Joe asked.

"That's part of the fun." Zack brought his hands together in a sharp clap. "Also, it's why we're calling the project *Hide-and-Sneak.*"

The door flew open, and a handsome face peeked in.

"Hey, is this the movie thing? Sorry we're late. I was helping my bud Hal move out of his dorm, and there was all this traffic. We got held up."

The salesman's smile slipped off Zack's face at the interruption, but it soon reappeared. "As I was saying, welcome to *Hide-and-Sneak*."

This time he was cut off by a loud, metallic crash.

"Sorry!" a voice outside shouted.

Zack sighed, looking around at his audience. "Okay," he said. "I suppose we might as well start by introducing the McGuffin."

3 The Phantom of the Marina?

"Who's this McGuffin?" Joe Hardy asked as Zack stepped outside. "An actor? The stunt coordinator?"

Kerwin shook his head. "You'll see."

A second later two newcomers came staggering in, carrying a large piece of metal junk.

At least that was what it looked like to Frank Hardy. Somebody had welded together a bunch of steel rods and balls into something five feet tall, that was very hard to move around. The two guys almost dropped it twice just getting it through the door.

"Hey, Hal, watch it!" The guy who'd first poked his head through the door said as he managed to keep the ugly thing from crashing to the floor. He grinned at the girls. "I'm Andy Slack," he said. "Everybody calls me the Slacker. And this is my best bud, Hal Preston."

Zack paid no attention, his eyes on the large, ugly metal construction. "This is the McGuffin," he announced.

"And what's that?" Trisha asked.

"I guess you're not fans of Alfred Hitchcock." Zack gave them a superior smile.

The girls shrugged.

"Hitchcock was a director of mystery films, a cinematic genius, I'd say, and I know Ms. Athelney will agree with me." Zack smiled at the businesswoman. "Whatever caused the mystery or action in Hitchcock's films, he called the McGuffin. It could be a clue, a person, an event—"

Or a really ugly thing, Frank finished for him silently.

"In our film this is what you'll be looking for," Zack said. "First you'll have to find it; after that you'll be searching for whichever team has gotten hold of it. Tomorrow evening bring your boats to the Bayport Marina. You'll get a package of charts and . . . other things that should lead you to where the McGuffin will be hidden. Find it, keep hold of it for three days, and bring it—well, clues about what you

18

should do with it will be in the package for you too."

"What about filming?" Willow Sumner asked.

"Yeah," Chet said. "Lines and things."

"There's no script." Zack looked as if he were above such things. "Our film will be improvised. Each boat will have one of us along as camera-person." He turned to the girl with the clipboard. "Melody, I suppose you should go with the girls."

Zack then turned to Andy and his friend Hal. "I'll be with Andy here. That leaves you with the other guys, Sprock."

Joe looked at the tall, bony guy. "Sprock?"

"It's a dumb nickname," Leonard ("Sprock") Kerwin growled, "from the days when film had sprocket holes."

"We'll all be using digital cameras," Zack said. "They're much more handy, which will be good, since the whole film is going to be shot on Barmet Bay." He sent another toothy smile toward Ms. Athelney. "Just like the first film of that famous Polish director—"

Frank tuned out. Apparently, what's his name was another favorite of the woman who was putting up the money for the film, but even she looked a little embarrassed at the way Zack kept kissing up. Ms. Athelney fidgeted in her seat, running a hand through her shoulder-length brown hair. Her restless hand, with a glinting gold and ruby ring, had revealed her right ear for a moment. A bare ear. No earring.

That's funny, Frank thought. *Shiny gold watch, shiny gold necklace—but no shiny earrings?*

Maybe she lost them, Frank thought, and glanced around the floor. Anything was better than sitting and listening to Zack's voice.

"So, there you have it," the would-be film genius finally said. "You'll have a day to get your boats ready. We'll meet at the marina tomorrow evening at six. You'll tie up, get your packages, and decide on a course. The next day at noon we'll set off, and we'll be filming to see if you guessed right and whether you get caught."

"The boats have to stay overnight at the marina?" Andy Slack said. "Who's gonna pay for that?"

"Already taken care of." Zack shot another cheesy smile at Ms. Athelney.

He's spreading it pretty thick, Frank thought. From the look on Melody's and Sprock's faces, they agreed with him.

Maybe Joan Athelney also agreed, but her serious expression didn't give any emotions away. She looked at her gold wristwatch. "I think that covers everything," she said, "and I have a meeting. Good luck to all of you."

With a nod to everyone, she left.

Zack looked around, realizing he'd been subtly upstaged. Ms. Athelney had effectively ended the meeting. "I'm sure we all have lots to do."

"Yeah," Sprock Kerwin said, clearly trying to keep a grin off his face. "Lots."

Taking their cue from Zack, the filmmakers left. The eight kids in the room looked at one another for a long minute.

Hal ran a hand through his dark, spiky hair, shooting a frown at his pal. "This sounds like one of those dumb reality shows on TV where they make people jump through hoops."

"Except there's no prize," Joe added.

"What are you talking about?" Chet demanded. "We'll be in a feature-length movie."

"Yeah, a movie with no script." Christy O'Hara smirked. "I wonder how writer girl with the clipboard liked that tidbit of information."

"Better for us," Trisha Eads said. "No lines to learn."

"Yeah," Chet said quietly. Frank could see the wheels turning in his friend's head. Without a script the camera would end up pointing mainly at whoever gave the best performance. Chet probably thought his TV experience would be a plus.

Willow Sumner tossed her hair over one shoulder.

Looks would count too. "So," the girl said to Andy, "what kind of boat have you got?"

Andy's face broke into another grin. "We've got a bunch of them," he said. "My dad's a fisherman—"

"And he figured you'd be helping him out now that you decided to ditch college," Hal said.

"He gave me the summer to explore choices." Andy glared at his buddy. "I'd say this is an interesting choice."

"How about you guys?" Trisha said, walking over to Joe. "What kind of boat do you have?"

"Oh, the *Sleuth*'s a great boat!" Joe said, but he yelped as the toe of Frank's shoe caught him on the ankle.

"Whoops, sorry," Frank said, collecting his brother and Chet. "Yes, we've got a great little boat—and a big job getting it ready by tomorrow evening."

Joe was still complaining about Frank's interruption the next evening. "I can't believe you kicked me!" He glared at his brother.

Frank rolled his eyes and turned toward Chet. "How are you doing with the sleeping bags?"

Chet climbed aboard with three bulky nylon sacks. "Last load."

A full moon rode the clear skies overhead. Its light was bright enough to read by. Frank opened the package they'd been given. "Let's get down to business."

The first thing they found was a folded map of Barmet Bay with some odd squiggles drawn on it.

"I still say we could have just tailed that loud-mouth Zack. It would have saved us a lot of non-sense." Joe squinted at the next sheet of paper. "Oh, great. It's marked 'Clues.'"

He began reading:

> To find McGuffin, sail Barmet Bay.
> Exactly where, we cannot say.
> You'll know you've gotten where you oughta
> All's quiet and dead in the water.

"Poetry?" Frank said in disbelief.

"Bad poetry too." Joe handed over the sheet.

"I don't like that 'dead in the water' part," Chet said.

"Nowadays, when people say something's dead in the water, it usually doesn't happen," Frank explained. "It's sailor's slang, an expression that describes when a ship's engines don't work or if there's no wind for the sails."

"Well, I spent the whole afternoon tuning up our engines." Joe laughed. "And when it comes to wind, the bay usually has more than people want."

Frank and Chet nodded. Barmet Bay had a reputation for sudden squalls.

As if in answer, the breeze off the water began picking up. Most of the docked vessels around them were sailboats. Riggings began to clang against tall aluminum masts. The marina filled with an echoing, ghostly sound.

"We're going to get a great night's sleep with that racket," Joe growled, grabbing the chart so it didn't blow away. Frank was still looking at the clue list.

> *You'll know exactly where to pick it,*
> *A watery graveyard—that's the ticket.*

"More cheerful clues," Chet said, furrowing his brow. He bent over the map. "You see any cemeteries down by the bay?"

"No, because your head is blocking the light!" Joe shifted the map. "Somehow a beach doesn't sound like a good place for a graveyard. One good storm could wash everything away."

His finger went to an island at the mouth of the harbor. "But I think there's a grave here on Merriam Island. They buried the old lighthouse keeper out there. It was a story on the news awhile back."

"We might be looking around the lighthouse,"

Frank said slowly, "but for a different reason. Some of those squiggles on the map look like sunken ships, don't they?"

"Yeah," Joe said, squinting again. "There's a big cluster of them near the lighthouse. I guess that's why they built the thing."

Chet nodded. "To warn people off Barmet Shoals."

"Yeah. But there are rocks around the lighthouse too," Joe said. "We almost tore the bottom off the *Sleuth* out there once."

"It's not as bad as Cape Hatteras," Frank said. "People called that the Graveyard of the Atlantic."

"'A watery graveyard,'" Chet said.

Joe leaned forward. "Where a lot of people probably wound up 'dead in the water.'" The pieces were fitting together.

"That gives us two possible, and fairly dangerous, places to go looking." Frank cocked his head for a look at the map. "Any other places marked?"

"There are a couple here and there." Chet bent over, his finger tracing along the map. "Whoa! Here's a whole crop of 'em!" Chet said.

Joe followed Chet's pointing finger. "'Shipwreck Cove,'" he read. "Nice name. There are coves all along the shores of the bay. How did the channel here nail so many ships?"

Frank tapped the map. "The only safe way in is

this narrow channel. Sea captains would steer for what looked like a safe place to drop anchor. Instead they'd smash into these sandbanks." He ran his finger along the shore. "Any other places like this?"

They scoured the map but found no more clumps of shipwreck symbols. "That leaves us three places to check tomorrow," Frank said.

"As long as we don't wrack up the boat getting there." Chet stretched to unkink his back—and froze.

"Uh, guys," he said, his voice dropping to a hoarse whisper, "don't look now, but I think somebody's spying on us."

4 Chasing Around

"Don't be stu—" Joe broke off as his eyes caught a hint of motion. He lowered his voice. "Hey, what's that? Two boats down, across the slip?"

Chet nodded, leaning over the map as if he were pointing something else out. "Thought I saw somebody ducking down."

"Let's get a little closer and see." Joe made a big production of stretching and yawning. "I think I'll go to the snack bar and grab a soda," he said loudly. "You guys want anything?"

"I'll go with you," Chet told him.

They swung over onto the dock, heading for shore and toward the boat where they'd spotted the intruder. It was a good-size sailboat. Joe jumped up onto the deck.

Suddenly, a dark figure sprang to the stern of the boat standing alongside.

"Run ahead, cut him off!" Joe yelled to Chet, who was still scrambling aboard.

Thudding footsteps on the dock told Joe that his friend was on his way. Meanwhile Joe charged along the narrow deck, then leaped off the front of the boat.

His speed carried his body across the gap to the next vessel. He hit the deck, staggered, and continued his mad dash as the waves slapped between the two boats.

Joe couldn't make out the shadowy figure ahead. Whoever it was wore baggy clothes that blended in with the darkness, and some kind of hat—

It was a baseball cap. Joe caught a glimpse of the visor as the intruder shot a glance over his shoulder.

Just then the spy tripped on something on the deck. While his running feet stumbled, Joe poured on the speed.

Chet must have seen what was happening too. "Hold it!" he yelled, rushing onto the deck.

His cry of triumph turned into a squawk as the staggering figure's knee connected with the side of his face. Chet tumbled sideways and landed in the water with a splash.

The intruder pulled himself together, swung down to the dock, and ran off at top speed.

Joe stopped at the prow of the boat, listening to his spluttering, splashing friend below. Sighing, he turned to find a rope.

For about the fifth time Frank said, "I don't get it. What was this spy supposed to hear? The rattling from these masts would drown out our voices."

Joe turned to Chet, who sat huddled in a blanket, sipping the cup of hot chocolate Frank had gotten for him. "You got pretty close to this character, Chet. Did you see who it was?"

Chet gave him a look. "All I saw was his knee. If I see it again, I'll definitely let you know."

"Nothing at all?"

Chet's hand went up to massage his cheek. "It was bony."

"Most knees are," Frank said. "Okay, so you didn't see, or feel, much of anything. How about your other senses? Close your eyes and think back. Did you smell anything?"

"Not till I got really close to the water," Chet answered.

"What was he supposed to smell on this guy?" Joe asked.

"For one thing, proof that maybe it wasn't a guy," Frank replied. "For instance, your new best friend Trisha Eads wears a pretty strong perfume, as I'll bet you noticed."

Joe was about to argue, but then he snapped his mouth shut. Could the intruder have been a girl? He tried to call up an image of the shadowy figure he'd pursued: baggy clothes, baseball cap . . .

"It could have been a girl," he said.

"A nice, healthy chase would be just the thing to get us all off the *Sleuth* and let *someone* get aboard for a little sabotage," Frank said.

"You've got a very twisted, untrusting mind, Frank," Joe remarked. "Speaking of twists, remember what Zack said? To expect plot twists?"

"I didn't see any cameras," Chet said.

"You're just hoping there weren't any cameras to catch your belly flop," Joe told him.

"They didn't need to film anything," Frank said slowly, shaking his head. "Just plant a seed in our minds for a payoff later."

"You mean, someone might be playing with our heads," Joe said angrily, "or setting us up?"

"Whatever our visitor was after—sabotage or plot twists—I think we shouldn't play his or her game." Frank smiled. "Let's just keep this among the three of us and see what happens." He yawned.

"Right now I want to turn in—unless you want to go looking for an all-night laundry to dry Chet's clothes."

"Just spread 'em out on the deck," Chet said. "We're not leaving this boat."

By the time Sprock Kerwin arrived with his camera, the early-morning sun had dried Chet's jeans and sweatshirt. The young cameraman immediately began filming Chet as he was explaining the whole hide and sneak idea to a woman on a nearby boat.

The woman was sitting cross-legged, working to splice two pieces of rope together. As her fingers deftly wove the fibers together, she nodded, shaking her gray pigtails. Large sunglasses hid her eyes. Joe couldn't tell if she was really interested in what Chet was saying or if her eyes were glazing over with boredom.

Kerwin turned from the scene, a look of pleasant surprise on his face. "Your buddy did a good job of explaining the film."

"Probably better than your pal Zack," Joe said. "I'm surprised he didn't have you filming his little speech the other day."

Sprock's face tightened. Joe had obviously hit a sore spot. "These cameras are the latest thing." The young filmmaker held out an amazingly compact little unit, changing the subject. "Easy to handle, supposedly easy to use. They'll work with whatever light is available." He sighed. "I hear that even beginners can get good results out of them, and I hope it's true. Zack ordered the top of the line, but they had to be shipped here. We only got them this morning. I had to teach the others how to use the stupid things while I was learning myself—"

Kerwin bit off his words, looking at his watch. "Almost time to get this show on the road." He aimed his camera at Frank and Joe. "I expect you've checked your packet and the map."

"Yeah," Joe said sarcastically. "I'm surprised you didn't draw a skull and crossbones in the corner."

Sprock stopped the camera and grinned. "Zack wanted to, but Melody thought it was too much."

Joe called Chet on board. Together they undid the lines holding the *Sleuth* to the dock.

Frank was already sitting behind the wheel. He put the key in the ignition and turned it slightly. The Chris-Craft's big engines beneath the deck throbbed to life.

Kerwin was already shooting film. "Just head out into the harbor," he said.

As Frank steered the *Sleuth* out, Joe spotted two other boats leaving the dock. One was a working fishing trawler, big and weather-beaten. The other was a very sporty jet boat, white with a bright red trim, and a folded-back red and white canopy.

"The competition, I take it," Joe said, nodding toward the two boats.

Sprock Kerwin nodded, panning his camera to take in the oncoming boats. "You can slow down here," he told Frank.

Seconds later the boats were in a ragged row just outside the marina.

Zack Harris clambered onto the deck of the fishing boat. He had his camera in one hand and one of those horns that work off cans of compressed air in the other.

"Ready!" he yelled across to the other boats. Sprock and Melody both were filming him. "Set!"

He raised the hand with the horn. It gave off an earsplitting blast.

Andy Slack's fishing boat took off so suddenly Zack staggered. For a second Joe thought the director was going to drop his camera in the water. Instead he lost the airhorn, letting go of it to clutch the side of the boat.

The trawler was on the rounded, tubby side, but it had good engines. They kicked up a white wake as Andy set a course for the mouth of the bay.

"Looks like he's heading for the lighthouse," Frank said, squinting in the sun.

"Either there or the shoals." Joe kept a careful eye on Sprock Kerwin as he spoke. But the cameraman kept a poker face as he continued to record what was going on.

"Maybe we should aim for a spot with less competition." Frank steered deeper into the bay.

The water was a little choppy, and the boat bumped a bit. Chet carefully made his way to the prow of the *Sleuth*. To Joe, Chet looked like a ship's figurehead.

Suddenly Kerwin swung the camera on Joe, so Joe figured he should look as if he were doing something. He picked up the pair of binoculars from beside Frank's seat. First he focused them on the rapidly shrinking trawler. As he started looking along the bay, he noticed another boat.

"We've got company," Joe announced.

With that distinctive set of colors, there was no mistaking the jet boat. It might look like an expensive toy, but Joe knew it could move faster than it was going. He focused in a little closer. The three girls on the boat had life jackets on—with additional fashion touches. Willow Sumner was acting captain. She wore an emerald green one-piece bathing suit that brought out the red in her hair. The blond girl, Christy O'Hara, wore a wild Hawaiian shirt as a cover-up. Trisha Eads was in a bright red bikini.

"We've got the 'babe boat' on our tail."

"I thought that's what you liked," Chet said, heading back to get a look. "Pretty girls in bathing suits."

"They're even chasing after you," Frank said.

"Guess they might figure on letting us do the dirty work of digging up the McGuffin, then stealing it from under us." Joe walked over to Frank's seat. "Let me take a crack at losing them."

Frank got up and let Joe take command of the boat. As soon as Joe was behind the wheel, he pushed up the throttle.

"They're speeding up too," Chet said. "Guess they know they've been busted."

"Bring 'em on," Joe growled. Gripping the wheel, he began easing the *Sleuth* through the water until it was headed directly for a small island. Actually this was more like a muddy rock with a couple of stunted trees growing out of it than an island.

Joe sped up the boat again. At the last moment he jerked the *Sleuth* aside. The island rock whipped past on their left. "Hope they weren't just concentrating on us," Joe said smugly. "Otherwise we may have a rescue on our hands."

"They came around it," Frank reported, "and they're closing the gap."

"Oh, yeah? Let's see how they like this." Joe sent the boat on a zigzag course. The powerful engines churned the water, leaving a huge white wake in their trail. Following them, the jet boat kept hitting the big, man-made waves. Joe grinned. "Maybe they'll get tired of having us continually slap their faces with water."

But the "babe boat" continued on their trail in spite of every one of Joe's maneuvers. The far shore of the bay was coming into view now. They were getting close to Shipwreck Cove.

"These girls just can't take a hint," Joe said. "Hang on, everyone," he yelled, spinning the wheel. The *Sleuth* swung in a tight circle until it was facing the other vessel. "Maybe a quick game of chicken will get the message across."

Joe's hand went for the throttle. Before he could turn up the boat's speed, the shrill whoop of a siren cut across the water.

5 The Long Arm of the Law

"Heave to!" an annoyed voice ordered over a loudspeaker.

Startled, Frank Hardy swung the binoculars around. He and Chet had been so busy watching the pursuing jet boat they hadn't bothered to look elsewhere.

As Joe killed the *Sleuth*'s engines, Frank thought: *Bad mistake.* The harbor police boat closed in on them.

"Busted," Chet muttered.

On land the Hardys had a solid history with the Bayport police. In fact, Frank and Joe counted one officer, Con Riley, as a friend. One look at the grim, sunburned face of the officer climbing aboard, and

Frank figured that his past friendships with local officers wouldn't count for much.

"That was quite a show you put on," the officer said admiringly to Joe. "Very impressive stunts. What are you doing, making a movie?"

"Actually—" Sprock Kerwin started.

The cop cut him off with a glare. "Turn the camera off, son."

The student filmmaker did as he was told.

"You were operating this vessel at an excessive speed," the officer said, "not to mention recklessly disregarding the rights of other boaters in the area."

That was the moment the girls chose to drift by in their boat at a sedate pace. Frank was glad that their engines drowned out the girls' mocking giggles.

Still glaring at Joe, the officer didn't even seem to notice Willow, Trisha, and Christy. "Hmm," he said. "Considering that recklessness, I wouldn't be surprised if you'd forgotten several items for your own safety."

The harbor cop produced a piece of paper. "What do you say we just run down this little checklist, just to see?"

If the *Sleuth* was missing one item on the harbor police list, it would mean a ticket and a fine.

Frank had taken a lot of kidding from Joe and

Chet about getting the *Sleuth* completely ready. Now, he hoped his attention to the safety checklist was going to pay off.

"Considering it's your movie," Chet whispered to Sprock Kerwin, "would you guys pay for the violation?"

Sprock shook his head. "With the tight budget Ms. Athelney's got us on, I don't know where we'd find the money."

So far the harbor cop hadn't found a violation. He squinted. "I see you have four people aboard, all wearing life jackets."

Joe nodded. That was the law after all.

"But this boat can hold six passengers," the patrolman said triumphantly. "Where are the other two life jackets?"

Frank thought the officer was reaching a little. But the law was the law, and Frank had prepared for it.

"Right here, Officer." He reached into a storage space under one of the seats and pulled out two inflatable life vests.

"Hmm." If the cop's face hadn't been already sunburned, it would have probably turned beet red at this discovery.

The officer pressed on with his list. It wasn't just that the cop was supercareful; he was super*slow*.

Long minutes crawled by as he searched for some-place where they'd come up short.

"I wonder what Willow and her gal pals are up to now," Frank said as the cop inspected the rest of the boat.

Apparently Chet was thinking the same thing. He stepped around the harbor patrolman, to pick up the binoculars and turned them toward the shore.

Frank managed to intercept him. "I don't think the officer's mood would improve if he thought we were girl watching," he said in a low voice.

Chet blushed until he was almost as red as the cop.

At last the harbor cop reached the end of his list. The *Sleuth* had turned out to be fully stocked with safety equipment. He had no reason to issue a ticket.

That didn't stop him from giving them a stern, and long, lecture on safety. Joe listened with down-cast eyes. Frank thought his brother was probably annoyed with himself for his stunt sailing—or for getting caught.

At last the harbor patrolman finished. "I hope you'll show better judgment in the future," he said. "By way of encouragement, you might remember that we'll be keeping an eye on you." He glared at the four boys. "Understand?"

"Yes, sir," they mumbled.

"Good." The officer got back on the patrol boat, swung it around, and pulled away.

"Hey, look," Frank said, nodding toward the cop. He could see the red-faced officer aiming a pair of binoculars at them.

At last the cop turned away. Chet snatched up the binoculars and scanned the shore. "I don't see—wait! There's a big hole in the sand!"

"Forget the beach," Joe said. "Check that out." He pointed to a small boat.

A girl in shorts and a T-shirt—she looked like Melody Litovsky—was standing on the bow of the jet boat, filming. The other three girls were clustered in the rear of the vessel, struggling to get something stowed behind a pair of seats.

"Three guesses what that could be," Sprock Kerwin said, nodding toward the girls. He too was operating his camera. Now he turned it on the boys. "What now, gentlemen?"

"I'll bet they've got the McGuffin," Frank said slowly, "but that doesn't mean they get to keep it."

Chet blinked. "What do you mean?"

"He means we can do what they intended," Joe replied. "They were going to let us dig the thing up, then tag us."

Frank nodded, heading for the wheel. "There's only one channel in or out of the cove, remember?

That's why there are so many wrecks. Well, I'm going to plant us right in the middle of their only way out." He carefully consulted the chart so that he would avoid the dangerous sandbanks.

Chet grinned. "With us blocking the way out, they'll have no choice but to turn over the McGuffin."

Still busy with their lopsided metal prize, the girls didn't even notice the boys' boat.

Melody finally turned, still filming. She suddenly swung the camera toward the girls, giving them a warning.

The McGuffin got one final kick from Willow before she and her friends dashed for their seats. Willow cranked up the boat's engine, a little too quickly, Frank thought. The engine sputtered for a moment before it caught. With Melody crouched in the tanning pit in the nose, the jet boat took off.

Frank's hand automatically dropped to the throttle. He was ready to move the *Sleuth* to cut them off in the channel.

But the girls didn't aim for the channel. They went straight for one of the sandbars!

"Get some ropes!" Joe looked torn between worry and annoyance. "We're going to be pulling them out of the water."

"Where was that medical chest again?" Chet asked.

Frank focused his binoculars on the speeding boat. *It's like watching a car accident happen,* he thought.

Just then the prow of the jet boat hit the sandbar, throwing up a huge spray. The vessel jarred up, shot across the barrier, and landed in deeper water with a splash.

Through his binoculars Frank got a clear view of the rear end of the flying boat. The impeller, the part of the engine that provided the thrust for the boat, stuck straight out of the stern.

Unlike the *Sleuth,* the jet boat had no propellers sticking down, nothing to catch on the sand. The bigger Chris-Craft would get caught on the sand, but clearly, the girls' boat wouldn't.

Trisha stood up to wave good-bye as the "babe boat" took off. Sighing, Frank put down the binoculars and began backing through the channel.

"Hey!" Chet exclaimed. "They're coming back!"

Frank killed the throttle and turned around. Joe, Chet, and Sprock all were in the stern of the boat, staring ahead. Willow Sumner was looping her jet boat around. The boat seemed aimed right at the *Sleuth.*

"What's she doing?" Chet asked in disbelief. "Playing chicken?"

"Not quite," Frank replied. "I think this is payback for Joe's throwing them our wake before. Now they're going to zoom past and splash us."

The jet boat was moving fast enough to raise a white rooster tail of water in its wake.

"We're gonna get soaked," Chet said.

The jet boat was close enough now that they could see Willow Sumner's pretty yet gloating face.

"She's cutting this awfully close," Frank said with concern.

Christy O'Hara must have thought so too. She looked worried and started to say something to Willow, but the helmswoman turned and shot her what seemed like an angry reply. Unfortunately, her jerky movement made the wheel on the girls' boat turn slightly. Willow whipped around, so the boys could see that her face had become a mask of horror.

Now the jet boat wasn't going to splash past. It was going to crash right into the rear of the *Sleuth*!

6 Going Up?

Joe Hardy made a desperate dash for the *Sleuth*'s controls, but Frank was already there. "Don't stall on us now," Frank muttered, gripping the throttle and pushing it forward. The engines roared into life beneath the deck, sending the boat flying forward.

Joe staggered, and Chet nearly fell, while the jet boat with the girls shot past, just inches from the *Sleuth*'s stern. Joe turned back just in time to see the other boat fly by and to get a stinging spray of water in the face. He shook his head to clear his eyes.

Chet, equally drenched, stood beside him. "I don't mind the water," he said, "but they didn't even say sorry for almost crashing into us.

them?"

With a snarl of disgust, he shook the water off the binoculars.

Sprock Kerwin had taken the spray on his back. He'd turned away to protect his camera.

"Didn't want to record the crash?" Joe said, trying to lighten the mood. "I hope you got a shot of Frank saving our sterns."

"It will probably come out looking like a very chaotic, jumpy pan," Kerwin said sourly. "Very unprofessional. I won't even know what I caught."

Curiosity aroused, he took a laptop computer out of one of the storage lockers and connected the camera. While Frank navigated through the channel, turned the *Sleuth* around in the cove, and headed back into the bay, Kerwin rewound the camera and replayed the tape.

"Nothing," Sprock reported after looking over the last shot. "Everything's just a blur on the tape. Nothing useful at all."

"That's about what we've got," Joe said, scanning the bay with the binoculars. "Willow and her buddies tore out of here. I was able to see what they were up to until one of those islands came between us."

Frank immediately directed the boat toward the island Joe was talking about. It was one of the larger ones in the bay, with plenty of bushes, and a grove of trees. Now that it was high tide, most of the island was under the water.

A quick circle around the island showed nothing, and there was no hint of a boat in the bay beyond.

"We'll have to go in closer and take a better look," Frank said.

Joe got into the bow of the boat. "Plenty of rocks and driftwood around here. Better move carefully."

He watched for obstructions while Frank brought the boat in as near to the island as possible. Sprock scanned the island with his camera, but Joe wouldn't trust him to say anything if he spotted the girls' boat. Why would he?

Frank seemed to have the same idea. "Take the binoculars, Chet," he said. "We know they can get in closer than we can."

This time they gave the shoreline a thorough going-over, paying special attention to areas where half-drowned shrubs or tree branches might provide hiding places.

"Nothing, zip, *nada*." Chet shook his head. "So where did they go?"

Frank gestured across the water ahead of them. "There are other islands," he said.

They spent the next couple of hours hunting for possible hiding spots around the nearby islands.

They saw lots of scraggy trees and waterlogged bushes, but not a hint of the vanished jet boat.

In fact the only other vessel they spotted was the harbor police boat. Frank throttled back the engines. "Even if we had a reason to go racing around, that boat's presence would stop us," he said.

"Let's face it, guys," Chet said. "We've been suckered. Those girls have gotten away." A grin crept onto his face. "Unless, of course, Frank brought along some special emergency gear. What do you say, Frank? Have you got a hot-air balloon packed away under one of the seats? Or maybe the makings of a seaplane?"

"Just didn't think of it," Frank responded with a laugh. He became more serious as he turned back the way they'd come. "I see one way we could get an aerial view, though."

He pointed toward a tall cliff overlooking Shipwreck Cove. The boys looked up.

"We'd be way over the islands up there." Joe turned to Sprock Kerwin. "What do the rules say?"

"The rules are for me to interpret"—the young filmmaker paused in thought for a moment—"and I say that that would be a pretty decent place to get a good establishing shot of the whole bay."

Frank steered back toward the cove while Joe

aimed the binoculars at the cliff. "We're in luck," he said. "There's a stairway built onto the cliff face."

Chet took the binoculars and observed the zigzag of the stairs up the craggy cliff. "Great," he said without much enthusiasm. "It'll be just like climbing up to the fourth or fifth floor of a building."

"You can handle it, Chet," Joe told him. Chet was admittedly a bit out of shape.

"Yeah, but can those stairs handle *us*?" Chet took another long look. "They look pretty beaten up."

"Only one way to find out." Having made up his mind, Sprock Kerwin was raring to go.

Frank brought the *Sleuth* into the cove. Off to one side they found a set of private docks.

Joe wrinkled his nose at the smell of freshly waterproofed wood. "This looks brand-new," he said as he tied up the boat.

"Let's hope that goes for the stairs too," Sprock said.

They crossed a stony beach to the foot of the stairway. It was more rickety than the docks, but they could see that several stair treads had been recently replaced.

"Let's play it safe and spread out," Joe said.

"I'll be last," Chet promptly announced.

"And I'll be first," Kerwin said. "That way I can shoot the bay with my camera, then catch you guys on film as you climb up." His lanky legs began taking the steps two at a time.

"Whoa, Sprock, slow down," Joe called after him. "You'll wear yourself out before you get halfway up."

Kerwin showed no sign of needing this advice as he continued to climb at top speed.

Frank was the next on the stairs. "I have no intention of racing after him," he said. "We'll take this at a reasonable pace. Okay?"

"Fine with me," Chet replied.

Joe waited till Frank had made the first turn on the stairs, then headed up. When he reached the first landing, he leaned over and called to Chet, "Ready?"

"Yeah. Great. Wonderful." Chet started to make his way up.

Frank was as good as his word, climbing steadily without pushing the pace. Joe followed easily, although he began to feel a little tired after the first few flights. "How are you doing?" he called back to Chet.

"Okay." Chet panted. "Remind me never to try one of those Stairmaster thingies the next time we're in a gym."

"As if I could get you into a gym." Joe laughed. He peered upward. "Good news. Only three more flights. Sprock is on the last one now."

"Good news?" Chet croaked.

"Well, you don't want to be on these things after sunset, do you?" Joe asked.

The sun had been low in the sky as they'd turned back from the islands. The shadows on the cliff face were getting darker and darker, while the top of the stairs was bathed in brilliant orange light.

Up above, it was bright enough to see Kerwin make it to the top of the cliff. Sprock turned his back to the sun and brought up his camera to get a panoramic view of the bay. Joe could see him leaning against the handrail of the stairs as he began shooting.

Just then a shadowy figure tackled the film-maker, and the two forms disappeared behind the cliff top.

7 Always Expect the Unexpected

The moment Sprock Kerwin disappeared from sight Frank charged up the last flight of stairs. Joe and Chet were doing their best to catch up.

Frank quickly reached the top and saw two figures rolling and struggling. He jumped on top of them, figuring he'd hold both down until the others arrived.

It didn't take long for Frank to be able to identify which of his prisoners was Sprock Kerwin. Frank wrapped his arms around the other guy and wrenched him around just as Joe threw himself into the fight.

"Help me hold him!" Frank gasped. He managed to get one arm, and Joe got the other, just as Chet appeared.

Their prisoner was still trying to tear loose. At the sight of a third antagonist the man lashed out with his foot. The toe of his shoe caught Chet right in the gut.

When Chet finally got his breath back, he let out an outraged howl. "What's the matter with you, Prito?"

Frank and Joe both stared. Sprock Kerwin's attacker—their prisoner—was indeed Tony Prito.

"Let go of me!" Tony yelled, and the boys released their holds. Tony looked around. "Frank? Joe? Chet?"

Then he turned to Kerwin, who had retrieved his camera and gotten to his feet. "Help me get this guy before he gets away!"

"Whoa, Tony! Cool down." Frank stepped between his enraged friend and the filmmaker. "What have you got against Sprock?"

"He's trespassing!" Tony shouted. "Remember my telling you how some of my dad's crew saw an intruder on the work site? I thought it was all a lie until I spotted this guy a couple of minutes ago."

Frank looked puzzled. "Where did you spot him?"

"By the general contractor's field office." Tony turned into the sun and pointed.

Now that his eyes had adjusted to the glare, Frank saw that they were standing at the edge of a huge construction site. Trailers and earthmovers were parked around several large holes in the ground.

"Looks like quite a project," Frank said. "Exactly where did you spot this 'intruder'?"

"I came around the corner of this shanty." Tony pointed to a modest trailer. "That's where they change their work clothes, wash up, and stash some of their tools. I saw this creep outside the general contractor office."

He pointed to another trailer, which was larger and more elaborate than the first one. It had a big red logo and a sign reading MATLING CONSTRUCTION.

"He ducked behind a backhoe, and I lost him for a minute. Then I spotted him trying to get down the stairs."

"Tony," Frank said gently, "Sprock had just come up those stairs."

Frank turned to Kerwin. "Is your camera okay?"

"Yeah," Sprock said gruffly. He stabbed a finger at Tony. "No thanks to him."

"Sprock, meet an old buddy of ours, Tony Prito. Tony, Sprock is one of the people making that film you didn't want to get involved with."

Realizing he had made a mistake, Tony apologized. Then something occurred to him. "Wait a minute!" he said. "Maybe I saw someone else, who's still around."

"We'll help you look, Tony," Frank told him. "We just have to take care of a few things first."

While Sprock was getting his establishing shot, Frank stood on the clifftop, scanning every inch of the bay with his binoculars. He spotted the jet boat in another cove that jutted out from the bay. The girls were struggling to get the boat's canopy up, and Frank got a clear view behind the back seats. The McGuffin wasn't there anymore.

Frank carefully checked the beach along the cove. No trace of any recent digging. And Zack Harris's metal monstrosity was really too heavy to be lugged very far.

"I wonder where it is," Frank muttered, turning the binoculars over to Joe.

"Until we know where it is, there's no sense tagging them," Joe said, staring down into the cove. "Besides, they aren't going anywhere. Trisha is passing out food. It looks like they're going to camp on their boat." He shook his head. "You'd think they'd want to sleep on the beach. Then they could enjoy a campfire. . . ."

Joe's voice faded, and he turned away. "Let's help Tony with this search, then get some sleep." He gave Frank a sinister smile. "I may have an idea of where to find the McGuffin, but it's going to mean a very early morning."

They searched the work site until there wasn't enough light anymore. "I tell you, I saw a guy!" Tony insisted. But even he began to sound as if he had doubts.

They made a fire pit and cooked themselves a meal with food they had packed on the boat. Tony then let them spread their sleeping bags in his dad's trailer.

Before sunrise the next morning Joe woke the others. After checking that the girls' jet boat was still in place, the boys had a hurried breakfast and buried the fire pit.

Once on the *Sleuth*, Joe changed out of his sweatshirt and jeans and into a rubber surfing suit. "I thought this might come in handy," he said. "Let's see if I was right."

While Joe collected a few more items in a net bag, Frank started the engines. In only a few minutes they'd reached their target, the other cove. Frank killed the engines and let the *Sleuth* drift. Joe slipped on diving fins and a mask and put a snorkel in his mouth. He slung his bag over one shoulder, slipped into the chilly water, and began swimming into the cove.

Even though he was wearing the surfing suit, the chilly water seemed to suck the warmth right out of his body. Joe kicked and stroked as quietly as possible through a gray, predawn haze. Ahead he spotted a darker shape: the "babe boat."

Joe took a deep breath and dived. Once he was underwater, he pulled a waterproof flashlight out of the net bag and shone it around. Okay. There was the anchor line, running up to the boat. And on the other end . . .

His lips curled into a grin around the snorkel mouthpiece. Bingo! There was the McGuffin. The girls had hidden it by using it as an anchor.

Joe swam over to the McGuffin and reached into his bag again. This time he brought out the two extra inflatable life vests that Frank had stashed away on the boat. Joe attached them to the McGuffin and pulled the tabs.

The vests filled out like balloons. They didn't make the ugly sculpture float, but they made it a lot lighter. Joe took out a knife and began sawing at the anchor line.

The McGuffin soon came free, and Joe swam with it toward the mouth of the cove. Even with the help of the vests, the metal monstrosity was an awkward burden. Joe's lungs burned.

Holding on to the McGuffin with a rope, Joe surfaced for air. He needed three air breaks before he reached the *Sleuth*.

His friends and his brother, waiting eagerly for Joe, tossed him a line. He tied it to the McGuffin. The boys had the prize aboard before Joe managed to pull himself onto the deck.

Sprock Kerwin ran back and forth on the deck, trying to record the action and casting anxious glances at the rising sun. "This camera is supposed to work in low light," he muttered, peering through the view-finder. "Heck of a way to test it, though."

Chet grinned. "Do we give the girls a wake-up call? Or—"

He was cut off by sounds of sudden commotion echoing across the water.

"They were anchored close to a sandbar that was hidden under the water at high tide," Joe said. "To judge from the sounds, they just drifted into it."

A second later they heard the jet boat's engine start, sputter, and die. Joe put a hand to his ear. "I'll bet the first blast jammed them farther onto the sandbar, and they can't start again."

"Maybe we should take a quick spin past them," Frank said, starting the *Sleuth's* engines.

The crew of the jet boat began waving and calling for help—until they recognized the other boat.

"I'd say this team got the McGuffin fair and square," Sprock Kerwin shouted over, filming the tousled girls. His fellow filmmaker Melody grabbed up her camera and began recording too.

Joe jumped up onto one of the seats on deck, waving. "Later, girls," he shouted. "It was real!"

Frank headed the boat up the bay, toward the ocean. Chet was still laughing. "That was priceless," he said, turning to Sprock. "Could I get a copy of that clip?"

"It gets better," Joe said, turning up the volume on the harbor radio receiver. "The girls are sending out a distress signal!"

Frank shook his head. "All they have to do is wait until the incoming tide floats them again."

Frank started changing their course. "I was heading for Bayport to hide in the boat traffic around there. Now I don't think we want to be too close to the harbor police."

Chet nodded. "After talking with Willow and her friends, they might suspect us of getting the girls into their mess."

"So, do we find ourselves another inlet or go right down the bay and catch lunch in that little town—"

Joe abruptly grabbed the binoculars.

"Trouble?"

Joe's face was grim. "You wouldn't expect a fishing boat in this part of the bay, would you?"

"Not at this hour," Frank replied.

"Then I think there's definite trouble. We've got a trawler heading our way."

"Andy and his pal?" Chet asked.

"Can't tell. Those fishing boats all sort of look alike." At that point Joe spotted a redhead sticking out of the cabin, pointing a camera their way.

"There's Zack," he reported. "Maybe they were just heading down to check out Shipwreck Cove when they heard the SOS from the girls."

"I guess they sped up to see what was happening," Chet said.

Joe nodded. "Anyway, looks like they've spotted us."

"No trouble." Frank pulled the *Sleuth* into a tight turn. "That boat's a tub compared with ours. We can outrun them."

Suddenly the radio crackled to life.

"Harbor police, this is powerboat five-six-three-K-three-H," Willow Sumner's voice came from the speaker. "We're off the sandbar, and we're trying the engine again."

Sound travels far across water. The boys could hear the snarl of the jet boat starting.

"All right," Frank said. "Now we've got trouble."

Joe nodded. The boys might have the McGuffin at that moment, but they were caught between two other teams that wanted it, too.

8 Abandoned Ship?

"Looks like this is where we live up to the title of your movie, Sprock," Frank said coyly. "*Hide-and-Sneak*. Brace yourselves, guys." Frank pushed the throttle forward.

The engines bellowed in response, and the *Sleuth* shot forward, leaving the fishing trawler behind.

The mouth of the cove where the girls' boat had been stranded was still ahead of them. As if on cue, the red and white jet boat appeared. It immediately began charging toward the *Sleuth*.

Frank veered away. In a straight-out race, he'd still bet on his Chris-Craft, but in the confined waters of the bay the jet boat was more agile. It could cut tight corners and go closer to the islands than larger boats. The jet boat continued to speed toward the boys.

Can't outrun them, so we've got to lose them, Frank told himself.

An island rose in front of them. Frank steered around it, then changed course, aiming for another island.

He managed to get the new island behind him before the jet boat cleared the first one. The roar of the other engine checked for a moment, then started again.

Joe handed the binoculars to Chet. "Let us know whenever you see one of the other boats. If we see them, they'll probably see us."

Joe knelt beside Frank, spreading out the chart of the bay. "There're a bunch of little islands coming up on your left," he said.

Frank steered left, but the "islands" were a disappointment. They had just a few straggling bushes. No trees, nothing that would really block the other teams' sight lines.

If one of the other boats came along now, we'd be spotted, Frank thought.

"Go on through," Joe said, rattling the map. "There should be bigger islands a little farther along."

"There's only one problem with going this way,"

Frank replied. "Sooner or later we're going to run out of bay."

"I see Andy's boat," Chet suddenly said. "And wait, they're turning."

Frank kept their boat on course to the bigger islands Joe had mentioned. He swung the boat around to hide behind the first island he found, and killed the throttle. "Okay. They won't be able to see us for a moment or two," he said, reaching for the map. "Let's see—"

The roar of the jet boat's engine was coming clearly from the other side of the island.

They're able to get closer in than we can, Frank reminded himself. He hit the throttle, spinning the wheel.

They darted back and forth among the islands. Some were large, some small. It was like some sort of nightmare geometry test, a constantly shifting set of triangles. Every time Frank managed to ditch one boat, he wound up being spotted by the other.

Twice he tried to turn around and head back up the bay. Both times Andy cut him off.

That guy may not have the fastest boat in the world, but he sure knows how to handle it, Frank thought.

On the other hand, Willow Sumner kept appearing from places she really shouldn't have been able to reach. She was getting pretty reckless, obviously determined to get revenge for Joe's trick with her anchor.

By the time she tags us and takes McGuffin, Andy will be close enough to tag her and take it, Frank thought. Still, he didn't want to give up and meekly hand the prize over.

Frank pulled behind yet another island, the last in the area. The next stretch of the bay was just open water.

"Take the binoculars and see if you can spot any other traffic," Frank told Joe.

A second later Joe was back. "We've got two boats," he reported. "Off to the left is the tourist ferry, heading back to the Bayport docks."

Then he pointed almost straight ahead. "There's a good-size yacht out there. I can't figure out if it's anchored or just lazing along."

"So," Frank said, "two possible hiding places. One moving toward Bayport, the other standing still—or close to it."

He glanced at Joe. "Which would you choose?"

"The moving one," Joe answered promptly.

"Hmm. I think we should go for the other." Frank started the engines again. "Sprock," he called over his shoulder, "another rules question."

The cameraman came forward, still shooting the action. "What's up?"

"We've got a yacht ahead of us. It's big enough to hide behind. Can I put a lookout aboard it so we can see if it's safe to sneak back into this maze of islands?"

Sprock thought for a moment. "At the risk of sounding as though I'm taking sides . . . why not?"

The ship ahead slowly came into better view. It was a nice-size cabin cruiser, painted a perfect white.

Joe whistled. "That little toy cost quite a bit of money." He grinned at Frank. "Can you imagine how many little jobs we'd have to take to afford a boat like that?"

"By the time we got that much money, we'd be too old to run the boat," Frank replied with a laugh.

As they swung around the vessel's stern, they found a painting of a pirate flag: white skull and crossbones on a black background. Beside it large black letters announced the ship's name, *Jolly Roger.*

"Nice name," Joe said. "I hope that doesn't mean we're going to be boarded by pirates."

"*We're* going to board *them*—I hope." Frank reversed the engines and brought the *Sleuth* to a stop.

"Hello?" he called out.

No answer.

Frank tried again. "Ahoy, *Jolly Roger!*" He smiled at Joe. "Does that sound as corny as I think it does?"

Joe shrugged. "Doesn't matter. They're not answering anyway."

"Maybe something's wrong." Chet came forward and pointed to the rope ladder hanging from the yacht's side. "I'll go check."

Chet's just trying to grab the spotlight, Frank thought. Then he shrugged. That was why they'd let Chet talk them into this whole crazy venture; so he could have his moment of film glory.

"Knock yourself out, Chet," he said.

A couple of quick maneuvers with the throttle and the wheel, and Frank pulled the *Sleuth* to within grabbing distance of the rope ladder. Chet kept a determined look on his face as he seized the ladder. Then he almost fell into the water.

While Sprock filmed Chet's climb, Frank and Joe kept their comments to themselves. Their pal had another moment of trouble pulling himself onto the yacht's deck. A moment or two later his head popped over the gunwale.

"There's nobody here," Chet called down. "There're all sorts of fancy computer controls. They seem to say the boat is just drifting."

Frank and Joe exchanged a look.

"I'll go check it out," Joe said.

Frank swung past the rope ladder again, and Joe began hauling himself up. He climbed much faster than Chet and swung himself aboard.

In a few minutes he reported back. "The cabins are empty, and it looks as though this sucker slipped its anchor. Weird."

His eyebrows drew together. "Hey, Sprock! Is this one of those plot twists Zack promised us?"

Kerwin gave a quick laugh. "I wish."

Joe shrugged. "Maybe we should change the name from the *Jolly Roger* to the *Marie Celeste*."

Sprock looked confused. "The who?"

"I guess you're not the biggest nautical trivia fan," Frank said with a grin.

Kerwin shook his head. "Neither was Zack, until that businesswoman began talking about the romance of the sea. Poor Melody wound up doing this whole pile of research so Zack could impress Ms. Athelney."

Sprock bit his lip.

I'll bet he feels he's giving too many inside secrets away, Frank figured. He decided to change the subject.

"The *Marie* or *Mary Celeste* is one of the great mystery ships of sailing history," Frank told Kerwin. "A merchant ship found it drifting along. All the crew and passengers were gone. There was a small, half-eaten meal on the table." He paused for a moment, then added, "We'll call this in to the harbor police—after we get away from here."

Frank called up to his teammates on board the *Jolly Roger,* "Come on back. Let's haul out—"

He was cut off by the whoop of a siren.

Oh, great, Frank thought. *Perfect time for the harbor police to catch up with us.*

9 The Financier

Chet Morton ran for the rope ladder. "We've got to get out of here!" he cried, panic in his voice.

Joe took his friend by the arm. "If they haven't spotted us already, the cops are sure to see us any second."

He gave his pal a lopsided smile. "I'd rather explain what we were doing here than why we were running away. Besides, if we're lucky, this won't be our sunburned friend from yesterday."

But luck wasn't on their side. The first face to appear over the rope ladder was sunburned and peeling.

Obviously the harbor patrolman had recognized

the *Sleuth*. His expression grew more grim as he got closer.

"We had a report that the owner of this vessel wasn't responding to calls." The officer took Joe by the arm and began leading him toward the bow of the boat. "Can you tell us anything about that?"

Joe noticed that the cop's partner was questioning Chet, and taking him in the opposite direction—out of earshot. This was a typical police tactic, separating the suspects during questioning.

"Look, Officer"—Joe squinted to get a look at the nametag on the cop's blue windbreaker— "Nelson. We're working on a college film out here. Hoping to get a better view of the bay, we pulled up beside this yacht and called to the people on board. When we didn't get an answer, we figured we'd better check it out."

"You didn't go into the cabins? You didn't touch anything?" Officer Nelson demanded.

Joe could feel the color rising in his own face. He fought down his anger before he said something stupid.

"Uh, Charlie?" The other officer interrupted. "Better take a look here. I brought this kid to the stern, and he spotted something in the water."

Joe looked across the surface of the bay. What

was that bobbing there? A head?

Officer Nelson grabbed the mike to his radio and began giving directions to the police launch.

In very little time the officers took off. The deck of the *Jolly Roger* gave Joe and the others a perfect vantage point to watch the ensuing rescue operation. As the launch returned and moved in toward the yacht, the head looked up, and a pair of frantically waving arms appeared. One of the crewmen, carrying a line, dived in. A moment later the harbor patrol had the body out of the water.

Soon after that the rescued man stood wrapped in a police issue blanket on the deck of the *Jolly Roger*. Frank and Sprock Kerwin were also brought aboard. Sprock was of course filming everything.

The man was probably average height, but looked shorter thanks to his stocky build. With his brown hair plastered to his head by water, it was easy to see that he was beginning to go bald. He had a small snub nose and a strong chin.

What struck Joe, though, were the man's blue eyes. They were piercing and sharp.

The man abruptly stuck out his damp hand to shake with Joe. "Pete Buckmaster," he said. "I understand I have to thank one of you young men for spotting me."

Joe had to work to keep his jaw from dropping. Everyone had heard about Peter Buckmaster, Wall Street's latest big moneymaker; the man they nicknamed the Buckmeister and the Buccaneer.

"Joe Hardy," he managed to say. "But the one you really want to thank is my pal Chet Morton over here."

Buckmaster pumped Chet's hand. "Son, I owe a lot to your good eyes," he said. "I brought the *Jolly Roger* into the bay last night and set the anchor." The moneyman's lips twisted into a grimace. "At least I thought I did. When I tried a morning swim, the yacht kept moving away on me. Began to think I was a goner."

"Don't you have a crew on board, sir?" Officer Nelson asked. Joe noticed his tone was a lot more respectful toward Buckmaster than toward the boys.

"Don't need one," Buckmaster replied. "This boat is mechanized and computerized up the wazoo. Sailing gives me a chance to get out and be alone. Swimming, on the other hand . . ."

He shrugged, and the blanket opened to reveal a soft middle. "Let's say I learned my lesson. I think I'll stick to sailing for peace of mind."

More engine noises filled the air. Joe looked over the side of the yacht to see the girls' boat and Andy Slack's trawler both bearing down on the *Jolly Roger.*

Joe turned to Officer Nelson. "Here comes the rest of our film crew now."

"Film crew?" Buckmaster asked.

Sprock Kerwin held up his camera. "It's a student project. We're filming an improvised chase situation here on the bay."

"A sailing picture, huh?" Buckmaster's voice filled with enthusiasm. "You don't see many of those nowadays. Are you the director?"

"Um, no," Sprock said. "The director's on board the trawler down there." Sprock pointed toward Andy's boat.

"What do you say we invite him and the others up?" Buckmaster said.

Things were moving a little too fast for Officer Nelson. "Mr. Buckmaster," he said, "what do you intend to do about these kids just climbing aboard your yacht?"

"Well, as you heard, I thanked them." Buckmaster sounded irritated. "Indeed I have to thank you, Officer Nelson, and the other patrolmen too. As soon as I'm done here, I'll get on the line to the local chief. What's his name?"

"Chief Collig," Nelson said, looking pleased.

Buckmaster nodded. "And I'm sure there's a police benefit fund where I can make a contribution?"

When he wanted to be, the big businessman was good at smoothing things over. Almost before Officer Nelson knew what was going on, he was climbing down the ladder to his boat.

Meanwhile, Pete Buckmaster was asking the crews of the other two boats to come aboard.

Zack Harris's thatch of bright red hair soon appeared over the deck line. The first words out of his lips were aimed at Sprock: "Does your team have the McGuffin?"

"McGuffin?" said Pete Buckmaster.

Clearly Buckmaster needed a more detailed explanation of what the "chase situation" was about. Interestingly, it turned out Buckmaster was a big Alfred Hitchcock fan, so their project was fairly easy for him to understand.

Buckmaster insisted on being introduced to everyone involved in *Hide-and-Sneak*. As he asked more and more questions about Zack's project, the filmmaker's natural enthusiasm took over.

Truly Buckmaster's interest was more than flattering. Dollar signs were dancing in Zack's eyes as he talked about the film. If a heavy hitter like Buckmaster got involved, Zack could expand his budget, and good-bye, Ms. Athelney.

"Shipwreck Cove, you say?" Buckmaster laughed when he heard where the filmmakers had buried the McGuffin. "I'm building a new house there. Maybe you saw the docks?"

Zack nodded.

"Sounds as though you folks will need to regroup," the financier said. "I'm sorry my rescue fouled up your plans. How can I make it up to you? Suppose you use my docks as your staging area? It's the least I can do."

Trying not to appear too eager, Zack agreed.

"I was heading to the cove now," Buckmaster said. "Why don't you kids come along? I'll give you the guided tour."

They all headed back to their boats, then followed the *Jolly Roger* back to Shipwreck Cove and tied up at the docks.

"There's enough room for a small fleet here," Chet said, looking at the big yacht and the smaller boats bobbing in the water.

A rope ladder came down the side of the *Jolly Roger*, and Pete Buckmaster made his way down.

The financier had changed into a designer sweatsuit, the kind that never actually sees sweat. He squinted as he looked at the stairway zigzagging up the cliff face.

"They told me the property had a wonderful view, but they didn't explain why. Remind me to talk to the architect about putting in an elevator."

"You mean you didn't see the place before you bought it?" Joe asked in disbelief.

Buckmaster shrugged. "That's what staffs are for."

He didn't need to go far for the architect. The moment he arrived on the building site, people came charging out of the trailers. The general contractor wanted approvals for several bills. The architect was waving complicated plans.

"We had to resite the two swimming pools," the architect said. He held out a sketch of a fancy building big enough to be a two-family house. "And you need to approve the design changes for the spa."

It was all a little much for Joe. But he saw that Zack, Mel, and Sprock were filming away as if there were no tomorrow.

More contractors and foremen appeared, and Buckmaster marched off to a meeting in the Matling mobile office.

"So much for the grand tour," Frank said with a laugh.

Willow Sumner sniffed. "I thought the mansion was all finished. Who wants to look at a bunch of holes in the ground?"

"I would." Joe turned to Frank and Chet. "What do you say, guys?"

"I didn't realize you were a construction buff," Chet said as they walked off to one side of the bustling site.

"I'm not," Joe whispered. "I just wanted to get away from that bunch."

Most of the area had been scraped down to bare earth. A little strip of grass remained along the chain-link fence that surrounded the property.

Joe led the way over to the grass so they could stretch their legs a little. The ground rose a little higher closer to the spot.

"You know," he said, "if we walk a little farther along, I'll bet we'd get a decent view of the whole site."

He was right. The fence cut across a hilltop where the boys could look down on the area they'd searched the evening before. Chet leaned back against the fence. "It would have been a lot easier looking for Tony's make-believe intruder if we— hey!"

Joe and Frank turned to find their friend lying flat on his back, on the other side of the chain-link fence.

"Leaving the property, Chet?" Joe asked.

"Hey, I just went to sit down," Chet said, scrambling to his feet. "The next thing I know, I'm out here."

Frank didn't find it so funny. He shook the fence, and a section of the metal mesh fell off.

"I think we can stop talking about make-believe intruders." Frank gently pulled on the loose section. The gap he created was tall enough for a good-size person to get through without even bending.

Frank let the section snap back. "I'd say a real, live person cut himself a private entrance."

10 Unhappy Ending

Frank held the slit in the fence open while Chet climbed back through.

"We'd better let somebody know about this," Joe said.

Frank nodded, leading the way back to the Matling Construction trailer, where everybody else was. A flood of people was coming out of the mobile office. As the boys neared the trailer, they could see a guy with a hard hat marked SITE MANAGER blocking the door.

"Sorry," the man said. "Mr. Buckmaster has moved from the construction business to just plain business. He's temporarily taken over my office."

Frank looked suspiciously at the manager. "That

seems a funny way to do things, even for a Wall Street genius."

The site manager shrugged. "It's the way he does things sometimes. I worked on another Buckmaster project and got kicked out of my own office several times. The guy lives on his cell phone. He's also got a whole office set up on his yacht, so he can do business wherever he sails."

Sprock Kerwin came over. "Where did you guys go? Zack just got a message from Mr. Buckmaster."

Zack was trying to play it cool, but Frank could tell that the film student was really excited. "Mr. Buckmaster—Pete—apologizes, but he's going to be tied up the rest of the day. I've decided to suspend shooting. Mel, Sprock, and I have work to do. We have a two o'clock meeting with Mr. Buckmaster tomorrow!"

Behind her glasses, Melody Litovsky's eyes gleamed. Sprock punched Zack on the shoulder. "Way to go!"

Zack turned back to his cast members. "Pete gave the okay for you to keep your boats at the dock," he told them, "and he's offering us lifts home."

"I could go for that." Joe stretched. "A nice, long nap in my own bed . . ."

"We'll meet here tomorrow at three o'clock,"

Zack said. "I hope to have some exciting announcements to make by then."

Joe was still chuckling over that as they got into one of the contractor's company cars. "Big announcements," he said. "Zack's probably hoping for a special effects budget that will have us playing *Hide-and-Sneak* on starships!"

"As long as he doesn't replace us with real—I mean, professional actors." Chet gave his address to the construction worker serving as their chauffeur.

"I don't think that's likely," Frank said. "Zack already has almost half his film shot."

They dropped Chet off, and then the Hardy boys were driven home to Oak Street. True to his word, soon after taking a quick shower, Joe hit the sack.

Frank, however, sat down in front of his computer. Once on the Internet, he did a Web search for "Buckmaster."

It was almost dinnertime when Joe stuck his head in the door. "Have you been Web surfing all the time I was sleeping?"

Frank leaned back in his chair. "I guess so," he said. "Found some interesting articles about our new friend Pete Buckmaster."

Joe laughed. "Zack's new friend maybe. So what did you find out about the guy?"

"It's your basic business story. He made a lot of people rich and got very rich himself in the process. Turns out he's a real film nut. He collects film memorabilia, like a sword from *Captain Blood,* a pirate movie, the hat some actor wore while playing a detective. . . . Here's a funny story about how he scored tickets for last year's Oscars." Frank brought up an article on his computer.

"You're usually not this interested in someone unless there's a crime involved," Joe said. "What's the dirt on this guy?"

"His marriage broke up about a year ago." Frank called up some more files. "Looks as though it got pretty ugly."

He glanced at his brother. "And there are interesting rumors flying around about Buckmaster right now. Seems as though his financial empire may be on shaky ground. Bad investments, bad management. Maybe he should spend more time in the office than on his yacht."

Joe shook his head. "Typical media nonsense," he commented. "First the reporters make a celebrity out of the guy; then they begin chipping away at him. After meeting him, I'd say Buckmaster is okay."

Frank shrugged. "We were with him for what, ten minutes? It's not hard to be a nice guy for that long."

"True." Joe took a deep breath. "Mmm, I smell

pot roast. I'll have a little of that, watch some TV, and then . . ." He yawned. "I think I'll catch up on a little more sleep."

The next afternoon Frank and Joe got into their van and headed to Chet's house. Their friend stood outside, waiting for the Hardys.

"So, do you think Zack will have a big announcement to make today?" Chet asked as he got in.

Joe grinned. "Maybe he'll tell us that *Hide-and-Sneak* will be coming to a theater near you."

"I only wish." Chet sighed.

They reached the edge of Shipwreck Cove, and parked the van against the chain-link fence. Then they went to the gate and gave their names to a construction worker with a clipboard.

"Over there," the man said, pointing to a spot inside the gate. Frank spotted the three filmmakers and Willow with her friends.

Zack Harris did not look as if he were full of great announcements. "Our meeting has been pushed back," he said. "Seems Mr. Buckmaster is working on something big."

"So we just get to hang out here," Melody Litovsky ran a hand through her sandy hair.

"Okay if we check out our boat?" Frank asked. Melody nodded.

"I guess those older models need a lot of mainte-nance," Willow Sumner said snidely.

Joe shook his head as he and his friends moved around the construction site to the top of the cliff. "Talk about high maintenance." He was clearly referring to Willow.

"I'm sure the *Sleuth* is fine," Chet said, as they reached the stairs.

"Not if people fool around with her," Frank replied. "I just want to make sure nobody was down on the dock, loosening wires—"

"Or messing around with the plug down in the bilge," Joe added.

"Plug?" Chet echoed. "Do you mean an electri-cal plug?"

Joe laughed. "More like a bathroom plug. It's something you pull when you want to drain water out of the bottom of the boat. Of course, if someone fools with it while the boat is still in the water . . ."

"Let's go check it out," Frank said.

Chet looked at the long walk down . . . and thought of the equally long walk up. "I don't want to get in the way. I'll wait here for you guys."

Frank and Joe headed down. A quick check of the *Sleuth* revealed no sabotage. As they tramped back up the cliff steps, Joe said, "I wonder if Buck-master told his architect about the elevator."

"It won't be helping us anytime soon." Frank took a deep breath. "We're almost to the halfway mark, though."

The stairway suddenly rattled with the sound of heavy footfalls coming from above.

Frank looked up. Was Chet coming down to join them? No, it was Peter Buckmaster.

"Hello," Frank said to the financier.

But Buckmaster was not in nice guy mode today. He brushed past the Hardys without a word.

After exchanging a look and a shrug, the boys continued up the stairway. Chet stood at the top, looking downward, confusion on his face.

"Did you get hit by 'Mr. Sunshine' too?" Joe asked.

"That Buckmaster guy is severely weird." Chet shook his head. "He came out of the trailer and got about three steps before his cell phone began bleeping."

"Did you pick up any stock tips?" Frank asked.

"Not unless 'yeah,' 'um,' and 'uh-huh' mean something special to you," Chet said. "Then his answers started sounding more like grunts, and his face went dead white. He snapped the phone closed and came whipping right past me. For a second, I thought he was going to take a running jump."

"But he decided to take the stairs instead," Frank said.

Chet nodded. "I decided to take a look and see what he was up to. As you made it closer to the top, he got into his yacht."

"Well, he's got an office setup in there," Frank said. "Maybe he needed a computer."

Zack Harris came hurrying over. "Was that Mr. Buckmaster who just flew past you? Did he say anything?"

The sudden roar of heavy engines interrupted the conversation. The four of them moved toward the cliff edge and looked down at the docks.

Below, the *Jolly Roger* shook in the waves, in spite of the lines still holding it in place. As the ropes tightened, they ripped the cleats off the dock. Finally free, the *Jolly Roger* began to pick up speed.

"The channel!" Frank burst out. "He's heading for the channel!"

From atop the cliff, it was easy to pick the safe way out of the cove. A thin bluish gray line stood out clearly against the yellow-brown of the sandbars.

But Pete Buckmaster wasn't taking the safe way out. He was hurling the *Jolly Roger* headlong onto one of the dangerous sandbanks. The yacht was no agile jet boat, able to hop over an obstruction. It stood deeper in the water than the Hardys' *Sleuth*.

Buckmaster's yacht hit the sandbar with a sickening, grinding crunch that could be heard clearly up on the clifftop.

The sound set Frank's teeth on edge.

But somehow, even as it tore its guts out, the *Jolly Roger* made it across the obstruction to deeper water. The yacht struggled on, rolling wildly.

Then something on board went up in a shattering explosion. The ship was consumed by a fireball!

11 A Quick Good-bye

An elbow caught Joe Hardy in the shoulder, temporarily distracting him from the fiery spectacle below. He turned to find Zack Harris standing beside him. The awed filmmaker had his camera up to his eye, recording the scene.

People came bursting out of the trailers at the sound of the explosion on the bay. The site manager tore into the Matling field office, then rushed for the stairs.

"Where's Buckmaster?" he demanded. "Where is he?"

"He—he's—" Chet gasped, pointing at the flaming, sinking hulk below.

"He took the easy way out," the man said bitterly. "After taking all of us for a ride!"

"What do you mean?" Frank said.

The site manager cooled down a little. "I keep the radio on while I work, the all-news station. They just had a big business report. Federal investigators moved in on Buckmaster's company. The customer accounts are all messed up, and nobody seems to know where all the money is. Millions of dollars may be missing."

The manager pressed his lips together. "One thing's for sure. There'll be no more dollars poured into this money hole!"

As word of the financial and explosion disasters spread, the site grew quiet. Contractors began to understand they weren't going to get paid for this job. Workers realized they'd be losing their jobs.

Very soon the backhoes and bulldozers began heading out the gateway. Contractors called their crews together and signed the workers out. A steady stream of people began heading home.

As the boys watched the construction workers leave, Zack beckoned Melody Litovsky over. "I need your car keys!" he said.

She stared at him. "Why?"

"I caught what happened to Buckmaster on tape! This is worth good money to the newspeople. I want to get the bidding started as soon as possible."

Melody dug into her jeans pocket and pulled out a key ring. Zack snatched it from her hand and ran for the gate.

"Well, goodie for him." Willow Sumner had come up in time to overhear most of what had been said. "Where does that leave the rest of us?"

Andy Slack and his friend Hal Preston joined the group. "If this rich dude is dead, and no one knows what's going to happen to his land, I want to get my boat away from his dock."

"I hope he didn't damage my dad's boat." Willow glared at Melody. "Or this flick will be more dead in the water than it already is."

Melody flinched, but she tried to defend her project. "You can't pull out now," she said. "Not when we've come so far."

Sprock Kerwin rushed in. "We'll definitely be going on with the film. And you all heard Mr. Buckmaster promise the use of his dock."

"Yeah," Trisha Eads said. "Until somebody else comes along and tells us to get out, that is."

Frank and Joe stayed out of the argument. Not surprisingly, Chet weighed in on the filmmakers' side. Melody and Sprock showed more diplomacy than Zack ever had. They convinced the skeptical kids to stick with the program and leave their boats at the dock, at least until a meeting with Zack the next morning.

"All right, then," Andy finally said. "Till tomorrow at eleven."

The group broke up. Willow and her clique headed for Willow's car. Sprock offered Melody a ride, and Andy and Hal went off to a beat-up old car.

Chet watched them march through the now-unmanned gate. "You think Tony is going to be showing up?" he asked.

Joe laughed. "What would he be guarding now? You think his father is afraid someone will get in and steal the dirt?"

Chet didn't answer; he just kicked a stone out of the dirt. "Are we heading out then?"

Frank frowned, looking off into the distance. A wall of ugly clouds was piling up at the entrance to the bay; it was a warning of bad weather coming in off the ocean.

"Looks like we've got a squall on the way," he said. "Maybe we should go down and make sure the *Sleuth* is safe."

Chet looked confused. "I thought that's what you were doing before the disaster."

"Now you know the true problem with older boats." Joe grinned. "They're even worse than Willow Sumner. Pretty, but *very* high maintenance!"

They headed for the stairway again. Joe turned to wave a joke good-bye to the now-deserted work site. From the corner of his eye, he caught sight of a shadowy figure darting behind the Matling Construction trailer.

"You're not going to believe this, guys," Joe whispered. "But I think I just spotted our intruder."

"Where?" Chet demanded.

"Ducking behind the Matling mobile office," Joe replied.

"Chet and I will head straight for it, then swing around either side," Frank whispered.

Joe nodded. "Meanwhile I'll go along and see if I can outflank him."

The boys moved silently, crouched over, trying to stay undercover as much as possible. Just as Frank and Chet got into position, the rain clouds rolled in. Water began pouring down on them.

Huge raindrops created watery craters in the dirt around Joe's feet. In moments the construction area had turned into a sea of mud.

"Frank! Joe! He's heading—" A sudden gust of wind blew the rest of Chet's words away.

Joe spotted his friend slogging his way through the new swamp. Then, ahead of Chet, Joe saw another figure.

There's our pigeon, he told himself.

The intruder was having as hard a time as Chet moving through the mud. The bulldozers had scraped away just the top layer of soil, creating an artificial hill of dirt and construction debris by the clifftop. What the diggers had revealed was a layer of clay. Now, as Chet and the uninvited guest were discovering, rain turned that clay into something with the consistency of glue.

Chet began hopping around on one foot. "My shoe!" he yelled.

The trespasser grimly plodded onward through the mud.

Joe tried to figure out the guy's course. He seemed to be heading away from the gate. *The fence!* Joe thought. *This dude is heading for the cut in the fence.*

The problem was, the intruder was closer to the mock escape hatch than Joe or Chet.

The edge of the cliff was solid rock. Joe could run along that and along the grass by the chain-link fence. He could possibly outrun the creep and cut him off.

The only problem was getting to the cliff edge. The pile of bulldozed debris stood in Joe's way.

Dirt mud should be better than clay mud, Joe thought.

Every step he took caused a loud, sucking sound as he fought his way through the rain. The wind was cold and wet. The mound of topsoil, concrete chunk, wood, and other construction junk was squishy instead of sticky. In fact, as Joe floundered his way up, he found the stuff downright slippery.

Easy does it, he warned himself after falling flat on his face into the dark goo. *Almost to the top now.*

At least the pounding rain washed his face clean. He pulled himself to the summit of the debris pile and took a look to check the intruder's progress.

The guy was still stuck in the mud. Chet was falling farther behind, but Joe could still make it. It would be close, very close . . .

Just then the huge pile of junk beneath Joe shifted as a critical mass of the dirt became waterlogged. The mound began to disintegrate and started to wash away. It was like the mud slides on the hills in California. Except this mud slide was on a cliff . . . and it was going to drag Joe over the edge!

12 Cliff Hanger

Joe desperately thrashed his arms and legs against the tide of goo. In spite of his effort, the mud dragged him along. The ground under him was slippery; there was no place to hold on to.

Suddenly there was nothing under Joe's legs. He'd reached the edge of the cliff!

The ground here was rocky and broken up. A stone thrust up from the ground. Joe wrapped his arms around it and hung on for dear life.

A torrent of gooey mud washed over him, bringing with it rocks, chunks of concrete, and even a couple of pieces of lumber. Joe kept his head down and held his breath as the flood tried to tear him loose.

At last it stopped. Joe raised his face to be washed by the still-pouring rain. He felt as if he'd been trampled by elephants. Everything around him was still slippery, slimed with mud. How could he pull himself back up? His feet slithered on the slick rock, unable to find a ledge. He felt chilled to the bone, and his arms were starting to get tired.

"Help!" he yelled. "Frank, Chet . . . somebody!"

He heard nothing but the cold, blustering winds blowing in from the bay. He clenched his muscles, trying to will some feeling back into his hands before they lost all sensation.

When he saw the end of a board coming at him, his heart sank. *This will finish me,* he thought.

But the board didn't move on a new flow of mud. Instead it hopped and shifted as it came closer.

Joe looked up and saw Chet Morton at the other end of the piece of wood. Chet looked exhausted. Reddish mud stained his legs up past the knees, and he'd lost both his shoes. But with determination he pushed against the board, turning to yell over his shoulder for Frank.

Within minutes Frank was on the scene. Together, Chet and Frank maneuvered the board to a place where Joe could get first one arm around it, then the other. The two boys were now able to haul Joe to safety.

"Just happened to see you when that mound of stuff collapsed." Chet almost had to yell in Joe's ear for his voice to be heard in the wind.

"Thanks," Joe said, brushing himself off. "Thanks, both of you."

The intruder was long gone now, and the trip down the stairs just seemed too much to consider. The boys changed course, heading for the grassy patches along the edge of the fence to get to their van.

They all felt better once they were out of the rain, but Joe noticed that Chet seemed quieter than usual.

"What's the matter?" Joe asked Chet. "You're a hero. So what if you lost your shoes?"

"You really were great out there," Frank said with a nod of admiration.

Chet sighed. "Yeah, for the first time since we got involved with *Hide-and-Sneak,* I did something *worth* filming. And of course there was no camera there!"

"If Sprock had been there, he'd have probably been blown off the cliff," Joe said with a laugh.

"And I don't care how good those cameras are," Frank added. "I don't think they'd have filmed much in a Barmet Bay squall."

The Hardys dropped Chet off and drove through

the continuing downpour until they reached their home. A long shower, some hot food, and dry clothes helped Joe feel human again. Later on he and Frank sat in the living room, watching television. The local news broadcasts had shown Zack's tape several times. When the national news started, the boys saw another rerun of the tape. The death of a Wall Street bigwig interested the whole country.

Joe looked at his brother as the reporters switched to the more boring financial details behind the case. "Zack must have held up the network for a good chunk of change," he said. "They're trying to get as much mileage out of it as possible."

"That's the news cycle," Frank said. "They'll probably forget all about Buckmaster by tomorrow."

But as they drove to the construction site for their eleven o'clock meeting, Frank was proved wrong.

"Yikes!" Chet said as they pulled up in the van. The road outside the gate was clogged with news vans. As the boys walked closer, they saw camera crews jostling one another for the best views. Grave-looking reporters spoke into microphones.

"Here we are at the scene of the tragedy," a thin young woman in a red blazer said.

Nearby an older guy in a blue jacket was

finishing his story. "The man known as the Buccaneer lived large and died the same way. Accident? Suicide? All we know is that he vanished in a blazing ship, like a Viking funeral."

Joe rolled his eyes at that.

"We've got a real, live media frenzy," Frank said. "Everybody must be trying to get fresh tape for noon news."

He spotted Zack Harris standing inside the gate. Their director was talking with one camera crew. As the Hardys neared the gate, they had to pass a gauntlet of microphones.

"Are you working on the film? How involved was Mr. Buckmaster?"

"Did any of you talk to Buckmaster before he took his life?"

"How did he seem?"

Frank and Joe just kept their heads down and pressed on. For Chet, although he'd spent the most time on camera, facing so many cameras at once seemed to bring on a case of stage fright.

Finally the boys got through. The three of them were happy to put the fence between them and the news vultures.

Willow Sumner and her friends were next to arrive. The three girls looked happy to be in front of the cameras. But Willow, Trisha, and Christy really didn't have that much to say. They hadn't seen Buckmaster or his yacht. All they could describe was the sound of the explosion.

The cameras quickly turned on Andy Slack and Hal Preston when they arrived, but the boys met the reporters' questions with silly grins.

As soon as Zack had everyone together, he led the group away from the gate to where Melody stood. She had what looked like a new set of clue packets.

"Good news, people." The filmmaker's face showed that he was pleased with himself. "I talked to the folks who'll be going over Buckmaster's assets. They said we can keep using the docks for a few more days. Sprock is already hiding the McGuffin. Melody has the clues. We're going to go for another round of *Hide-and-Sneak,* this time for two days. Whoever brings the McGuffin to the secret destination wins."

Zack cleared his throat. "If we have a tie, like what happened around Mr. Buckmaster's yacht, we'll give the win to the team that holds on to the McGuffin the longest."

Willow nodded. "That sounds fair."

Sure, Frank thought. *Right now your team has the best record.*

Naturally Andy Slack, who had never even got a

hand on the McGuffin, disagreed. "Why not do another round?" he said. "A tiebreaker?"

"We really can't afford it," Zack said.

"Your budget should look a lot better after selling that tape to AmericaNews," Andy snarled. "You might think about springing for a prize—or paying us."

"I can see you have no idea about how filmmaking works," Zack said stiffly. "The postproduction costs—"

Luckily a rather sandy Sprock Kerwin arrived, breaking the tension. The three filmmakers went into a huddle. Andy and Hal stood off to one side, scowling. Frank had to smile when he saw the girls gravitate toward the cameras. He laughed when he saw Joe follow the girls.

"Typical," Frank said, turning to Chet.

"I didn't think Joe would be giving any interviews," Chet said with a smirk.

Frank turned to see what Chet was talking about, then laughed louder. One of the newspeople had managed to catch Joe.

"Toby Gregson," she said, holding out a microcassette recorder. That stuck out in this high-tech crowd. So did the way she was dressed: jeans and a checked shirt. Her graying hair was long and frizzy, unlike the carefully coiffed reporters in front of the cameras.

Must be a newspaper reporter, Frank thought,

moving closer to eavesdrop. Unlike the TV folks, Gregson asked some intelligent questions—especially when she learned Joe had been watching from the clifftop.

"Did you actually see Buckmaster board the *Jolly Roger*?"

"Well, no," Joe said. "We weren't looking. But he had to be on the yacht, didn't he?"

Toby Gregson leaned forward for her next question. Her hair shifted, revealing her ear.

Frank couldn't believe what he saw. He swung around and walked past Chet, straight for the filmmakers.

Zack was annoyed at the interruption. "Can't you see—"

"No," Frank cut him off. "There's something I need to see."

He turned to Sprock. "Do you have the film you shot the first day handy? I've got to see it now."

13 A Clue from the Camera

Sprock Kerwin looked a little surprised at Frank's insistence.

"It's important," Frank told him.

Sprock turned to Melody Litovsky. "Mel?"

She cleared the papers off the large silvery box they'd been using as a desk. It looked more like a metal-wall oversize suitcase.

Sprock set the case on its side and opened it. Most of the space within was taken up by sponge padding, which held the three cameras and the laptop computer Sprock had used. The rest of the box held cassettes of digital film.

Kerwin ran through these cassettes, checking labels. "Here's my first one," he said, putting a cassette in one of the cameras.

He handed the computer to Melody and took a cable out of the case. Then he shut the top again and retrieved the computer from his friend. Sprock rested the laptop on the silvery surface, connected it with the cable to the camera, and booted up. "Was there any scene in particular that you wanted to see?" he asked.

"Right at the beginning, when you were shooting Chet on the dock."

Sprock fiddled with the camera, typed in a couple of commands on the keyboard, and soon Chet's picture swam into view on the computer screen. Chet's voice sounded a little tinny coming out of the small laptop speakers, but that wasn't important.

"Okay, that woman Chet's talking to. Do you have a close-up of her?"

"Yeah, I tried, hoping for a reaction shot. Problem was, she wasn't giving me very much of a reaction."

Sprock fast-forwarded the camera. The image of the woman on the boat grew. Then the camera panned, moving from a full-face view to a profile.

"Hold it there." Frank leaned in, looking carefully. "So," he said, "I wasn't crazy."

"If *you* say so." Zack gave him a snotty look.

"What did you see?" Melody asked.

"That woman has a torn left earlobe," Frank

replied. "Exactly like the reporter who was just talking to my brother."

Frank rushed back to the gate. Now Joe was standing with Trisha Eads, trading jokes. Frank scanned the crowd. "Joe," he said, grabbing him by the arm, "where's the woman who just interviewed you?"

Most of the camera crews were clustered around the vans. There was no trace of the boys' reporter.

Joe looked around and shrugged. "Dunno." He looked in puzzlement at his brother. Frank turned around and walked over to Chet.

"What's with him?" Trisha asked, her eyes hinting suspicion.

I guess he'll tell us when he's good and ready," Joe replied. "One thing I know about Frank. When he gets that look, there's usually a surprise revelation on the way."

Joe went after Frank, to find him talking with Chet about jewelry, of all things.

"Hey, look," Joe said. "Trisha brought her own car. We're going to grab some lunch and hang out for a while. She's pretty decent, despite her choice of snobby friends."

Joe half expected a lecture about giving away secrets to the enemy. Instead Frank just gave him a nod. "Sure. Okay. I've got some work to do anyway."

Frank looked up from the computer monitor when Joe popped his head in the room.

"Just got in. Dinner's in five minutes." The younger Hardy gave his brother a curious look. "Mom said you wanted to eat early."

Frank didn't give any clues to why he wanted dinner early. Instead he asked, "How was lunch?"

Joe grinned. "Fun. I like Trisha. She's feisty. She doesn't put up with much, even from Princess Willow."

He gave Frank a knowing look. "Hey, we didn't even talk about *Hide-and-Sneak* if that's what you're worried about. As far as movies go, we were more interested in choosing a flick to go see tonight."

"Cancel your date," Frank told him. "I already talked to Chet. We're spending the evening at Shipwreck Cove."

"Ah, Frank—" Joe began.

Frank shrugged. "I guess I could always get Tony Prito. We're going to catch the intruder tonight."

"Ooh," Joe said, pretending to be wounded. "You really do know how to fight dirty. I'm in."

The sun was low in the sky when Frank parked the van. They were well away from the front gate and close to the chain-link fence with the secret entrance cut in it. They had a bit of a walk to get to their destination.

Chet started to complain, but Frank said, "We don't want to make our guest suspicious by parking too close."

Joe shook his head. "I don't know how you can be so sure he's in—"

"There have been people in there all day," Frank replied as they walked along the grass alongside the fence. "See? A couple of the construction trailers are already gone. Whatever's going on will have to be finished tonight, before the whole place is disassembled."

They slipped through the slit in the fence and began looking for hiding places. The good news was that the afternoon sun had been hot, baking the clay soil dry again.

"The idea is to choose a place to hide that gives cover from someone coming in," Frank said, "and going out."

By the time they were set up the sunset was at its peak. Frank had already warned his friends not to talk. The intruder shouldn't know they were there until it was too late.

Now came the hard part of the stakeout: the waiting. Frank found himself looking at his watch again and again. The third time he really got annoyed with himself.

You're not supposed to be paying attention to your watch, he told himself.

Frank scanned the area. Even though he knew where the others were hiding, he couldn't spot them. Good.

Chet's head popped up, and he took a look around. At Frank's hissed warning Chet ducked down again.

Taking care that his own head wouldn't be silhouetted, Frank went back to surveying the area. Nothing at the main gate. No suspicious shadows flitting around the remaining trailers at the site. Nobody heading their way across the roughly leveled expanse of clay. No one coming along the fence.

Figuring that he'd used up at least half an hour, Frank allowed himself to check his watch.

Thirteen minutes.

He sighed, shaking his head.

At that moment a pebble came flying down to hit Frank in the ankle. To judge from the direction, it seemed to have come from Joe's hiding place.

Cautiously Frank raised himself for another look. Although full darkness hadn't yet fallen, it took him a moment to make out the figure picking its way along the fence.

Frank picked up the pebble and flipped it toward Chet. The warning worked. This time he barely peeked out of his hiding place.

All was ready. Just a little more waiting.

The shadowy figure slipped noiselessly through the cut in the wire fence. Half crouched, the intruder looked back and forth. It was just dark enough outside that the boys couldn't make out any of the stranger's features.

The trespasser rose slowly and took a couple of steps forward.

Come on, come on, Frank silently urged. *One more step . . . two . . .*

The dark figure finally obliged, setting off the trap. Joe rose from his hiding place and ran to block the way out.

Chet jumped up, turning on his flashlight. "Hold it!" he shouted.

Frank had to give their adversary full marks on guts. Unable to retreat, the intruder charged forward and broke past Chet.

That was Frank's cue. He got up and shone his flashlight directly into the running figure's face.

"Nice to see you again, Mrs. Buckmaster," he said.

14 Mrs. Who?

"What? Who?" Joe couldn't believe Frank. His brother hadn't given any hint of this.

Joe and Chet quickly closed in on the intruder. Their flashlights helped them see whom they had cornered. The intruder took off her baseball cap and shook out her hair. It was shorter than Joe remembered, and much less gray.

"You!" Joe exclaimed. It was Toby Gregson, the reporter who'd interviewed him.

Chet's beam was aimed directly at the woman's face. "I talked with you at the marina. But you were wearing sunglasses."

Frank nodded. "As I said, you've met Mrs. Buckmaster before. In fact we all have; she was also Ms. Joan Athelney."

The woman gave them a "so what?" shrug. "Sara Buckmaster," she said, sticking her hand out at Chet. "I'm sorry about what happened on the boats. I stumbled, and your head got in the way of my knee."

Chet shook hands with the woman. "It's okay. I lived."

Then she turned to Frank. "You must be the older Hardy brother."

"Guilty as charged," Frank said. "But you had the advantage of research. I managed to put together the clues about who you were only this afternoon. In the husband and wife interview you did for *Lifestyles Monthly* you mentioned the riding accident that left you with a torn earlobe. I'd already seen that on Toby Gregson and the woman on the sailboat. And I remember how Joan Athelney was loaded with jewelry—except for earrings." He shook his head. "The names should have told me something."

"Told you what?" Chet asked.

"Tobias Gregson and Athelney Jones were Scotland Yard detectives in the Sherlock Holmes stories," Frank said.

Sara Buckmaster gave them another shrug. "I always liked those old mystery stories better than the movies Peter made such a fuss over."

Frank nodded. "I guess your husband is the reason for all this fuss."

"I've been trying to catch up with him ever since he drained our joint accounts and dumped me a year ago," Mrs. Buckmaster said.

"He's been living on his yacht for the past year," Joe said.

"Hiding out there," Sara told him, "dodging me. I didn't have the money to hire detectives, so I had to track him down myself."

"To do that, you had to become the Woman of a Thousand Faces." Frank had to hand it to the woman for being clever.

"Yeah, you're also the Phantom of the Bayport Marina," Chet added.

"Yes, I'd been looking around the marina at night," Sara said. "Pete might have been docking there."

"And your involvement with the film? Why?" Frank asked.

"It seemed like a good way of getting next to Pete. I was sure he'd go for a movie that combined boats and a sculpture. But funding the film was expensive. Those college kids were using up the last of my money. I decided it would be worth it, though, for a chance at Pete."

"I guess there's no chance of that now," Joe said.

"Are you so sure he's gone?" Sara asked.

"I saw his yacht—" Joe said.

"But you didn't see him *on* the yacht, right?" Sara interrupted. "That's why I came around here today. I needed to hear if he was on the yacht from an eyewitness. Did any of you actually see him on the *Jolly Roger*?"

All the boys had to admit they hadn't.

"So you think he wasn't on that yacht when it went up?" Joe asked.

"I'm saying it happened at an interesting time," Sara replied. "It was just after the feds raided his office and found that millions of dollars were missing."

Chet laughed. "You think Pete has a treasure chest full of hundred-dollar bills?"

"Maybe a briefcase full of thousand-euro notes," Sara replied. "There are also smaller, more valuable items that you could fit in a lunch bag. If I could find where he stashed his loot, I could really hurt him."

Frank raised an eyebrow. "Another reason for the film scam and getting aboard his yacht."

"It seemed like the obvious place to look," Sara said in her defense. "At least till it blew up. I've tried looking around out here, but this site is too big. Can you guys suggest any places where Pete spent a lot of time?"

"The mobile office for Matling Construction," Chet answered promptly. "That's where he usually was."

"An office?" Sara looked doubtful. "Seems like there'd be an awful lot of people going in and out."

"Yeah, but it's a whole trailer," Chet said.

"One that could be wheeled out of here at any moment," Frank noted.

"But it's still here now," Mrs. Buckmaster said. "I guess it's worth checking out."

"That won't be so easy," Frank said. "It's sure to be locked."

Joe grinned. "We could take a look at it, see what we could do."

"Technically it wouldn't be breaking and entering," Sara said. "We're trying to recover stolen property."

Frank wasn't convinced of that, but he went along with the others as they headed for the Matling trailer.

Joe examined the lock. "Not too easy, but not impossible," he announced, taking some small tools from a case. It required a little work, but soon the door was unlocked and swung open.

"I have a bad feeling about this," Frank said, but he followed the others into the trailer. The interior was pretty crowded, with two desks, filing cabinets, a pair of computer terminals, and chairs for meetings.

"Briefcases!" Chet announced, pointing to a rack with several bags.

"Kind of out in the open for hidden millions," Joe said. He picked one up. "This one isn't even locked."

They checked all the briefcases but didn't find any money. No other suspicious cases turned up, although they searched pretty thoroughly.

Sara crawled out from under one of the desks and brushed off her knees. "A bag of gemstones would take up a lot less room," she said. That set them off on a new search for nooks and crannies. They found a lot of dust, several lost pens, and someone's secret stash of candy—but no secret fortune.

"This is getting us nowhere." Mrs. Buckmaster finally had to admit. She bit her lip in frustration.

"Maybe he really did feel like he just messed up and couldn't bear to face the consequences," Frank said.

"You wouldn't say that if you really knew him," she replied. "He always planned ahead. When we broke up, he had a whole program laid out to get me out of his life."

"Which didn't exactly work," Frank replied.

Sara Buckmaster's face tightened. "It came close enough."

She turned away and looked blindly out the window of the trailer. "I can't shake the feeling that he's out there somewhere, laughing, waiting for things to die down a little before he picks up his ill-gotten gains and disappears into the world again."

Frank stood beside her. "You might believe that—"

He broke off, staring at the last thing he expected to see on the abandoned construction site: the beam of a flashlight, coming from the gate!

15 Unwelcome Guests

Joe stepped over to the window to see what Frank was looking at. "Speak of the devil?" he whispered. The oncoming gleam vanished for a moment, hidden by the bulk of one of the trailers. When it reappeared, the light had split in two. To judge from the way the beams bobbled over the rough ground, there had to be two intruders.

"If that *is* Pete," Sara Buckmaster muttered, "who's with him?"

As the lights came nearer, they heard a familiar pair of voices arguing.

"So, dude, if we're going for a big payday, why not try for the whole enchilada?"

Hal Preston's drawl was unmistakable, and a second later the boys heard Andy Slack's voice. "Well, duh, there's only two of us and three boats. Besides, it would be harder to sell that big Chris-Craft. The jet boat, though, that'll go fast."

"Yeah, but think of those wannabes standing on the dock," Hal said. "That Melanie chick going, 'Zack, man, our fleet is gone!'"

"Melody," Andy said with a laugh. "Yeah. Snob-girl Willow will eat Zack alive if anything happens to Daddy's boat."

The pair continued their banter until they were right outside the trailer.

"We can't let them do this," Frank said.

"We don't have to get involved." Sara reached into her jacket pocket. "I've got a cell phone. We can call the harbor police—"

But Joe was already opening the door. "Yo, dudes," he said, "why don't you just head home and chill?"

Andy shook his head. "That Zack guy needs a lesson. He dumped all over my ideas, wouldn't listen. He's got money, and he won't share."

Hal gave the boys and Mrs. Buckmaster a puzzled look. "So, what are you doing here? You going for a payday of your own?"

Frank now stood on the wooden stairs leading to

the trailer door. He was soon joined by a reluctant Chet and an even more reluctant Sara.

"This is Mrs. Buckmaster," Joe said. "We're trying to help her find something that belonged to her husband."

Andy responded with a nasty laugh. "Big rich guy, lots of big talk. 'Maybe I'll help with this film.' 'Move my swimming pools over there.' And he was really broke all along!"

"Look." Frank impatiently came down the stairs to stand in front of Andy. "Whatever you were going to do isn't going to happen now, because you've got an audience. Why don't you—"

"Why don't *you* get out of our way?" Andy had worked himself into a rage. His hand went to his belt. A second later the flashlight beams were reflected in a long fisherman's knife.

"Move it," Andy demanded, "or I'll gut you like a fish!"

"Great," Joe mumbled, jumping down to the ground. Chet slowly started walking down the stairs.

In a move almost too quick to follow, Frank's hand fastened on Slack's wrist. He hauled Andy's arm out straight and pivoted, twisting and applying pressure with his other hand.

Andy yelled with pain. His hand twitched, and the knife went flying to the ground.

"Martial Arts 101," Frank said, pushing him away. "How to deal with loudmouths waving knives."

Andy might have lost his weapon, but he was still furious. Roaring, he hurled himself at Frank. Hal followed suit.

Joe flung himself forward and tackled Hal. Andy's friend went down, but on his way he managed to clip Joe. Hal quickly got to his feet and threw a punch at Chet.

Bad move. Chet was a peaceful guy, but he knew how to fight when he had to. He hunched, taking Hal's wild swing on the shoulder. His counterpunch caught Hal in the gut and folded him in half. By then Joe was on his feet, and he grabbed Hal's arm and twisted it behind him. Andy Slack still lay on the ground, thanks to Frank's martial arts expertise. The fight was really just about over when a pistol shot rang out.

All the boys whirled around to see a white-faced Sara. Standing behind her, holding a pistol to her head, was Peter Buckmaster!

"That was just to let you know I've got a gun," he said.

And a hostage, Frank thought.

"So why don't you all be smart and get on the ground? Sit on your hands."

Everyone followed Buckmaster's instructions.

Frank knew how hard it would be for him to get quickly to his feet from this position.

"Very good," Buckmaster said. "Some of you don't seem all that surprised to see me. I'll bet I have Sara to thank for that. She always had a suspicious mind."

"I wonder why," Joe replied sacastically. "What are you going to do now? You can't keep us here forever."

"Hey, Mr. Buck*meister*, Hal and I will help you out," Andy Slack suddenly said. "We're capitalists, just like you, only on a smaller scale."

"Interesting," Buckmaster said. "Why don't you go find some rope?"

Andy came back with a coil of rope and began tying together each person's ankles and wrists. He jerked on the ropes that restrained Frank. Very soon the older Hardy began to lose feeling in his hands.

"Your friend too," Buckmaster said after Andy had finished with the Hardys and Chet. Andy followed Buckmaster's instructions.

"And now my wife, just the wrists."

Frank could only watch as Andy bound Sara Buckmaster as well.

"Good job." Their captor reached into his pocket and pulled out a large roll of bills. Andy stared at the money greedily, never noticing the pistol swinging around. It caught him in the side of the head. He went down like a sack of potatoes.

Buckmaster tied up the unconscious Andy. "Not a very professional job, but it'll have to do. Now you know the first two rules of successful capitalism: Never do anything you can get someone else to do, and never pay for anything unless you have to."

"You still won't get away with this," Joe growled.

"I have so far," Buckmaster said coolly. He held up a fat leather bag. "Top-quality gems," he announced. "My rainy day fund. When I realized I'd have to sacrifice the *Jolly Roger,* I stashed it in the foundation of the house."

He shook his head. "And when I come to pick it up, what do I find but a bunch of boys fighting? With my dear wife as the audience! Sara will come along with me—at least for the first leg of the trip."

Frank didn't like the sound of that. "What good will that do you?" he asked. "You might have pulled off this whole operation if everyone thought you were dead. But your secret is out now."

"Who's going to believe a bunch of kids?" Buckmaster's laugh was like a snarl. "What proof do you have? Sara might have been able to convince people. That's why she's coming with me."

Pete Buckmaster began pulling his bound wife toward the stairway to the docks.

As soon as he turned his back on the boys, Frank and Joe began desperately trying to loosen their bonds, but Andy's knots held.

Of course he had to get a fisherman's kid to do the job, Frank thought bitterly.

No matter how Frank and Joe flexed and twisted, the ropes remained tight. They were beginning to lose all circulation in their hands and feet.

A strange scraping sound caught Frank's attention. He turned to see Chet bunch up his legs and push his body across the ground. Chet repeated this wormlike motion again and then again.

"What are you doing?" Frank asked. "Trying to scrape the ropes off?"

Chet shook his head. "I'm looking—"

He let out a sudden yell of pain. "Ow! I found it."

"What?" Joe asked.

"Andy's knife," Chet replied. "I thought it wound up over here, and I was right. It just stuck me in the rear."

16 Parting Shot

While Chet squirmed around, trying to grasp the knife without being stuck by the blade again, Joe and Frank wormed their way over to their friend.

"How are your hands?" Frank asked.

"I stopped feeling them about halfway over here," Joe answered.

"He really went to town on mine," Frank told Joe. "How about you, Chet?"

"Pins and needles, but I can still move them. Ha! Got it!" Chet twisted around. "Now what do I do with it?"

"We move back to back, and then you try to cut me loose," Frank replied.

Joe had often tried to cut somebody's ropes with

his own hands tied behind his back. It was difficult enough with practice, but this was Chet's first time. "Just try not to cut Frank," Joe said, trying to help.

"Yeah," Chet said, trying to look over his shoulder.

With a lot of contortions, a few yells, and a brief delay when he lost the knife, Chet worked and worked. Finally, with a triumphant cry, Frank tore his hands free.

He winced as he rubbed some life into his blood-starved hands. Then he leaned over, took the knife, and cut the ropes around his ankles. Frank then turned to Joe.

"Hey!" Chet exclaimed.

"His hands are almost as bad as mine," Frank said, cutting the bonds on Joe's wrists. He turned to Chet and cut him loose before cutting Joe's ankle ropes.

Hal Preston twisted around on the ground, looking up at Frank. "How about me?"

"I'm tempted to leave you here with your snoozing buddy," Frank said.

At that moment Andy gave a low groan. "Wha—"

Frowning, Frank cut the foot restraints on both of them. "I'm leaving your hands tied for now, but come with us," he said.

The boys rushed down the stairs to the docks,

although they knew there was no hope of catching Buckmaster. While Chet had been getting the knife positioned on Frank's ropes, the sound of an engine had come up from the bay.

Still, they had to try.

"Oh, man," Andy moaned before they were even on the last flight of steps. "My dad's going to kill me."

Frank could easily see why. The fishing trawler lay deep in the water—too deep. Its deck sloped down until it was about a quarter submerged, and they could see way too much of the rounded keel. "Must have knocked out the bilge plug," Frank said.

The *Sleuth* hadn't been sunk, but it had been cut loose. It was drifting away from the dock, following the tide out to sea.

The jet boat was gone.

Frank made a quick decision, cutting Andy's and Hal's hands free. "Get on your boat and see if the radio is working." He shook his head. "What a time not to bring my cell phone."

Joe ran down the dock and jumped into the water. "I'll try to catch the *Sleuth*!" he said.

Andy and Hal made their way along the deck of their listing boat and climbed into the cabin. A moment later Andy's head reappeared. "Radio's busted." He shook his head. "And waterlogged."

Frank watched his brother as he cut through the water after the drifting boat. "Then it's up to Joe," he said.

Joe Hardy climbed aboard the *Sleuth* and shook his dripping hair out of his face. Leaving a trail of water, he dashed over to the controls.

The front of the radio was smashed, and the microphone was gone. Whatever had been used to break up the radio had also been used to ruin the ignition.

"Great," Joe said through gritted teeth. "So it's either 'Good-bye, *Sleuth*,' and I swim back and let her drift, or—"

He stopped to examine the wreckage of the ignition, then traced some wires under the control panel.

This isn't the best thing to do when you're soaking wet, he thought. He took a quick look around and found a towel to dry his hands. Then he got some insulated tools and got to work on the wiring. It took some time because of the extra safety precautions he had to take. In a short while, though, he managed to bare the necessary wires and touch them together. The hot-wired engines roared to life.

Joe got behind the wheel and steered the *Sleuth*

back to the docks. "Buckmaster messed things up, but I got her working again," he shouted to the others.

"The radio?" Frank demanded.

Joe just shook his head.

Frank turned to Andy and Hal. "All right, you two. Remember what you promised."

The two boys ran up the stairs.

"What did they promise?" Joe asked.

"To call the cops at the first pay phone they reach," Frank said.

"You think they'll actually do that?" Joe turned to Chet. "You should follow them."

Chet stubbornly shook his head. "I got you into this whole thing in the first place. I'm sticking with you to the end."

Joe grinned. "Then hop aboard," he said. "We've got a jet boat to catch."

Joe stayed behind the wheel and swung the *Sleuth* out of Shipwreck Cove and into the bay. He spotted the faintest phosphorescence in the water, the remains of a boat's wake, and set off in that direction.

Soon, Joe sighted the jet boat. But even his best steering efforts couldn't bring them any closer.

If only the wiring hadn't been damaged, he thought. *If we had managed to get free just a few minutes earlier . . .*

Frank came up beside Joe. "We're not going to catch them, Joe."

"No," Joe said, with a hint of disappointment in his voice.

Frank pointed off to the left. Bright lights glared on the water. This was where the *Jolly Roger* had gone down. Several harbor police patrol craft clustered around the site. "If we could get them to help . . ."

"How?" Joe demanded. "We have no radio to call for help. Anyway, by the time we convince them, Buckmaster will be out to sea."

"You think he's getting away?" Chet asked Joe. He turned to Frank. "Too bad you didn't include a couple of emergency rockets, Frank. With some of those, we could at least take a shot at him."

Joe jumped as if he'd been slapped. "Rockets!" he repeated. "Frank, take the wheel!"

He went to the hatch that led to the engines, calling over his shoulder, "Chet, we've got a gas can on board. Try to find it. And get some rope."

A few minutes later, can in hand, Joe siphoned some fuel out of the *Sleuth*'s tank into the container. Chet had tied one end of the rope to a cleat at the rear of the boat. Now he was tying the other end around the handle of the can. Joe rummaged in a locker, looking for one more thing.

"Here it is," he said, opening a heavy-duty plastic case. Inside were a flare gun and an emergency flare. "One rocket, coming up!" He broke the gun open, put in the flare, and snapped it shut. "Okay, Chet, let her go."

Chet threw the fuel can into the *Sleuth*'s wake. The rope went taut. Now the can was bouncing along behind them like a tiny water-skier.

Joe rested the flare gun on the stern of the boat. "Wish me luck," he said. "We get only one shot."

17 Naval Maneuvers

The flare gun bucked in Joe's hand as he pulled the trigger. Like a bolt of searing brilliance, the burning flare whizzed across the water just like the rocket Chet had wished for.

It hit the can dead on. The flash was pretty impressive, the noise was even better, and the burning trail stretching behind them was the icing on the cake.

As if in response, sirens suddenly whooped, and the harbor police boats roared into action.

The patrol craft quickly caught up with the boys' boat. "Heave to!" an amplified voice ordered. "I repeat, heave to!"

The face over the bullhorn was familiar: Officer Nelson, surely redder in the face than ever.

Joe shook his head, pointing ahead to the almost invisible jet boat. "No—over there!" he yelled.

"What?"

Shouting himself hoarse, Joe managed to get across the fact that there was probably a fugitive in a stolen boat up ahead.

There was a moment's silence. Then Nelson said, "If this is part of your stupid film . . ."

Just then, two of the patrol boats roared past. One stayed with the *Sleuth*. "Just in case we're lying," Chet said with a smirk. Officer Nelson shouted something incoherent into his radio.

The *Sleuth* fell farther and farther behind the chase. But the boys were able to see a police helicopter come clattering out of the sky and throw a spotlight on the fleeing jet boat.

The jet boat was still in the lead as the *Sleuth* reached the mouth of the bay. Just in time, a coast guard cutter appeared from behind Merriam Island, cutting the jet boat off from the sea.

Buckmaster might have been fearless in the stock market, but with all that firepower converging on him, he gave up without a fight.

Another harbor patrolman aimed a bullhorn at the *Sleuth*. "We've got Buckmaster and a woman.

Change course for the Bayport Marina. We'll need statements from you."

The boys arrived at the marina just as Sara Buckmaster was taking her first shaky steps on the pier.

"Well, you got him," Joe told her.

Sara rolled her eyes. "Doesn't look as though I'll see much money out of it." Her expression became thoughtful. "Unless there's a reward for helping recover some of the stolen assets . . ."

Frank spoke up. "I've been talking to one of the officers." He lowered his voice. "They were all ready to throw the book at us when a call came in reporting the theft of the jet boat."

"So Andy came through," Chet said.

Frank nodded. "And because of that, well, I thought maybe we could cut him some slack." He smiled. "Buckmaster gave that kid a pretty stern lesson."

"Not to mention his having his dad's boat sunk," Chet added.

The police whisked Sara and Buckmaster away. They took the boys' statements right on the pier. The marina was soon quiet again, except for the eerie clanging of riggings against the aluminum masts.

When the questioning was over, Joe, Frank, and Chet walked along the pier toward dry land. Joe noticed his pal's shoulders had begun to droop. "What's the matter, Chet?"

Chet sighed. "I broke my neck to get into this movie thing."

"And ours too," Joe added, jabbing Chet in the ribs.

"It was an adventure," Frank said.

"Yeah, but the best stuff I did was never caught on camera!"

Joe had to admit Chet had a point. He'd staged a daring rescue, found the knife that freed them, and cut Frank loose, and his rocket comment sparked the plan that got the attention of the harbor police. But Sprock Kerwin hadn't been around to record any of it.

"I think Sprock, Melody, and Zack will be even more bummed than you are," Frank said. "Not only did they miss a thrilling climax for their film, but their whole project has turned out to be a scam worthy of a Hitchcock mystery movie."

"*Hide-and-Sneak* is totally dead in the water," Joe said. "Andy's boat is ruined, and Willow's jet boat is in police custody."

"And the *Sleuth* will be laid up for repairs for a while," Frank added.

At the end of the pier Joe noticed a newspaper vending machine. "Hey, look," he said, "the new issue of the *Bayport Alternative* is out."

He got a copy of the paper and opened it. "I see the little theater group is looking for actors. They're doing *South Pacific*. Sailors, nurses—and you don't have to bring your own boat."

Chet looked at the article, then closed the paper. "I don't know . . ."

"What?" Joe said. "By tomorrow you'll be a local hero!"

"Yeah, who became one by sailing on the bay," Frank said.

"You'll be sure to get a part," Joe said.

"You think so?" Chet's eyes began to gleam. "Hey, I've got an idea! Let's all try out!"

The Hardys exchanged a swift look. "Nope, sorry." Joe shook his head. "I'm all acted out."

"Me too." Frank smiled at Chet. "Besides, if you're going to be a star, it's best to shine alone. Right?"

"Yeah," Joe said as they walked toward a phone booth to call home. "That's show biz."

BILL WALLACE

Award-winning author Bill Wallace brings you fun-filled animal stories full of humor and exciting adventures.

Published by Simon & Schuster

648-32